Praise for

"Vénus-Khoury-Ghata's spare, unflinching prose leads the reader to very heart of violence, to the essence of the unending struggle between liberty and submission, between social traditions and the freedom to love as one chooses." —*Le Monde*, France

"Musical and poetic, a powerful voice touched with grace." —*Le Figaro*, France

"How to give when you can no longer receive? How much should an outsider seek to disrupt? Who should cast the first stone? Vénus Khoury-Ghata gives her answers to these questions with all the elegance, lightness and empathy we have come to expect of her."
—*L'Express*, France

"A novel born of rage." —*Le Soir*, Belgium

"Vénus Khoury-Ghata's love for language runs as deep as her hatred of injustice and cowardice."
—*L'Orient Littéraire*, France

Seven Stones

Vénus Khoury-Ghata

Translated from the French
by Aneesa Abbas Higgins

JACARANDA

This edition first published in Great Britain 2017 by
Jacaranda Books Art Music Ltd
27 Old Gloucester Street
London WC1N 3AX
www.jacarandabooksartmusic.co.uk

Originally published in France by Mercure de France 2007,
under the title *Sept Pierres pour la Femme Adultère*

English edition arranged through The St Marks Agency

A CIP catalogue record for this book
is available from the British Library

Seven Stones has been produced with the support
of the Centre National du Livre

ISBN: 978-1-909762-63-3
eISBN: 978-1-909762-64-0

Jacket Design: Rodney Dive

Typesetting: Simon Collinson

Printed and bound in the UK

A mattress, a cooking pot, a goat.

She will leave them to the people of Khouf, with no regrets. It is the stones that prey on her mind, the pile of stones in the square. For her.

For her alone.

Which of these stones will be the first to strike her?

Which will end her life?

The mattress, the cooking pot, the goat. She will keep them until the final moment, the sheikh has promised her this. The sheikh is a man of his word.

Afterwards, things will run their course.

The mattress, the cooking pot and the goat. Her possessions will pass into other hands at sunset, for this is the time when stonings take place. Will her legs have the strength to carry her, she wonders, or will she have to be dragged along the sun-red-dened path to the heap of stones in the square?

A mattress of sheep's wool; a cooking pot seasoned with a century of grime; a tall, rangy goat. This is all she will leave when the men of Khouf come for her. They will shove her roughly towards the square to face the waiting drummer, and as the sun sinks rapidly behind the mountains he will beat the drum three times, three swift beats to echo the sun's haste and signal her execution.

The stones will rend the air and the women will seize her mattress, her cooking pot and her goat. They will sleep on the mattress, light their stoves beneath the pot and milk the struggling goat as it kicks against the sight of its owner being pushed towards the square where the drum and the setting sun await. For now, the fatwa that weighs on her has changed nothing of her life. She still has her mattress, her cooking pot, her goat. The change is wrought within her. She wonders what form her pain will take. Whether she will suffer once she is dead. She must not allow herself to think about this, it will serve only to increase her terror when the moment comes.

Her thoughts run on.

Her one regret will be that she will not have solved the mystery of why the moon waxes and wanes in the course of the month while the sun remains unchanged.

I.

Noor's sons have left; the village has turned its back on her. Her monthly flow has ceased, she no longer bathes or cleans her house. She is a ruin, she says, like her humble home, walls crumbling from neglect. In the evening, when the watch on her is relaxed, she calls; 'Zahi! Zad! Zein!', certain that the echo will bring them back to her. Zahi, Zad, Zein, three names. No road leads them to her, and with nowhere to go their names rise up in her mouth only to fall as dust on the ground. Noor feels brittle as the with-ered leaves that cling to the soles of her feet, dry as her well forsaken by water. She eats very little, lights no fire to ward off the cold that has seeped into her bones, tries to keep everything in its place. She moves her chair cautiously, as if it might cry out at her touch, fixes the position of her prayer carpet in her mind. She wants to feel the presence of her belongings around her when the men come to lead her to the square. When the shrinking sun surrenders to the grip of the mountain, they will come, with children, and mangy dogs to seize her goat and use it for the meal, to be eaten, as tradition demands, after casting the first seven stones, the stones that bring redemption. 'Seven', she says, counting on her fingers. Seven, like the days of the week, like the rocks that secure the roof of the warehouse. Seven stones to split her head open like a pomegranate ripened in the summer sun.

She will not be waiting for them, but she will know when to expect them. She will try not to panic when they come into view behind her Barbary fig. She will try not to blame them, for they will be the ones to put an end to her sorrow, her longing for Zahi, Zad, Zein, her sons not seen since she lost track of time. From her door, she sees only the red earth, bloodied by battles between wind and sand as they grapple for meagre scraps of grass. Wind and sand, red as Satan's tongue, staining everything in their path. Red, the colour of her goat's once white pelt, red, the colour of her sheet draped over the hedge, red, the colour of her hair, crinkled like dried corn husks. Wind and sand bring only menace now.

The fatwa has cut short her life, shrunk the space around her. Since the fatwa, she has been forbidden to enter the village. Now, everything has become a threat. The fog spat out by the mountain is a pack of wolves crawling on their bellies towards her. The sound of a plane flying over the sleeping desert is a giant wave. Once, she thought she saw the sea from her rooftop, but it was a mirage. Seven villages lie between her and the sea. What she thought was the

grey line of a wave was the single paved road linking the
desert to the coast.

Forty days, the sheikh decided, forty days. From the
night of the *khamsin* when she opened her legs to the
stranger, the man who mounted her as the wind howled
in every crevice and hollow of her defiled body. It is futile
to ask her if he loved her. She answers with another question: "Does the plough love the furrow beneath its blade?"
She tells you that no man had been near her for three sea-
sons. Her husband had left her, for his own niece, left her
with four walls and the children. Four walls to protect her
children from the *khamsin,* as it sank its teeth into their
little bodies and bit into the plump flesh of the Barbary fig.
No point in shouting at him, she says. He wouldn't listen,
would he? A look of doubt crosses her face. She is wary,
regrets having said so much.

'You want to write my story in a book? Is that why you're
interested in me?'

She turns her back on you, bends down over a bowl filled
with dirty clothes and starts to rub collars and sleeves furiously. You crouch down next to her and explain that you're
here to help her get the fatwa lifted. She does not believe
you. You insist, and with a brusque movement she spills
murky water on your feet, then throws you a cloth to dry
yourself with. It leaves a streak of blood on your skin and
you cry out. She takes the rag back from you, unfolds it,
mutters a prayer as she stares coldly at the blood-streaked
slop.

All at once, her anger subsides. She owes you an explanation, gestures with her chin towards the metallic knitting needle. Tightly knitted rows of stitches hang from its twin.

Two needles to knit a scarf for the winter, one of them to unknit the unborn child, you think with horror.

'You don't expect me to keep it, do you?' she protests vehemently. 'Better if it goes before me. Stones have no heart, adult or child, it's all the same to them.'

'You're pregnant?'

'Perhaps, perhaps not. I'm staying one step ahead.'

'You could get septicaemia, blood poisoning, it could kill you.'

'All the better for the hens, the stones in the square can be used to chase off foxes.'

You ask her if she remembers the date she was raped.

'You mean when he entered me from behind, gave me pleasure?'

She touches her finger to her temple and thinks before shaking her head sorrowfully. She does not know exactly what night it was. She only remembers the *khamsin* and the cat that hadn't come home. Zahi, Zad Zein were calling for it. She searched the village, her face covered by her *litham*, she miaowed hoping the cat would recognise her voice, it didn't have a name. Mewling as she walked, she battled against the wind that kept dragging her back. She leaned back against the wall of the brickworks, too tired to go on, she would have stayed there, swallowing needles of fire, if a jeep hadn't pulled up.

'The man signalled to me to get in.'

'Then he raped you.'

'He entered me, as he would his wife. And then took me back home, without the cat. Zahi, Zad, Zein saw it all and told Moha everything.'

Squatting on her thin legs, she scrutinises your face.

'Go on, say it. A *gahba*. I'm nothing but a whore.'

'I don't know what you mean', you say, thinking you want to tell her she's a fool, the queen of fools.

She says Moha took her sons away from her, that he left her the house but afterwards he'll take it back.

Then she utters the words that take your breath away:

'A *gahba* must be put to death, by stoning.'

She gestures, to make her words clear.

Is this the sheikh's voice speaking through her mouth? Or is it Noor's own voice, issuing from the depths of the body given to the stranger?

'They're dogs,' she chants rocking backwards and forwards. 'Men are dogs.'

'Did he come back the next day?'

'Every night, when it's dark, he comes back. In my dreams I hear him mewing at the door. I open the door. There's no one there.'

You're asking her about the man and she's talking about the cat. You want to save her life and she is doing her best to convince you there was no rape, that she was willing.

'Did the French send you?' she shouts at you, suddenly full of rage. 'Nothing but water on a burning stone! What do they bring us but a kilo of flour, a kilo of sugar, a kilo of rice and a blanket? Like a bone thrown to a dog! Your aid workers never shake our hands or dip their bread in our plates. They've never married one of our girls. They're here today, gone tomorrow, birds that pass in the night, flying by, faster than the *wakwak*.'

Her anger spent, she turns to you, asks if you've ever eaten cooked cactus leaves. Without waiting for an answer, she says you simply slice them thinly like beans, cook them with onions and oil, a dish fit for a sultan.

You were expecting to find a woman in despair at the prospect of being stoned to death, instead you are being told how to cook by an expert chef who wants to share her recipes with you.

Abruptly, her mood changes again, her voice ringing as she taunts you with accusations.

'You know nothing of our food, nothing of our ways,' she exclaims. 'I have betrayed my own flesh and blood, I must pay the price. You're wasting your time on me, what will be will be.' Seeing your dismay, she softens and tells you they won't be throwing stones at her until the drought is over. The ground is too hard to dig. All is not lost, she assures you, the fatwa may never be carried out. Someone will step in: an uncle, cousin, nephew. Someone must take charge of restoring the family's honour.

'And when I'm dead,' she adds, still trying to reassure you, 'I shall be beyond reproach, as blameless as the next person. Not a speck of dust on my feet. I'll even have the

Fatiha recited for me. But no *chawaheds* though, they are only for the faithful.'

'*Chawahed?* What's that?'

She is surprised at your ignorance and explains, as if she were reciting a lesson.

'Two stones face Mecca: one marks the dead person's head, the other, his feet. A woman who is stoned to death is not entitled to them. But she does have something people who die a natural death don't have. She is cut off from this world without ceremony, but she has the power to come back unannounced. Back to where she died. She works her way into all the things she left behind, her children, her prayer mats, her basil plants.'

She tells you of a woman named Zahia, buried in a shallow grave because there was no one to dig a grave of proper depth. She came back, made her way into her house, without forcing any locks or slamming any doors, and went back to the carpet she was weaving when she was interrupted by the sheikh and the drum. She changed the colour of the threads and wove a new design, to taunt them and show them she had returned. She took the green thread and replaced it with red, the colour of her blood not yet dried in the square. Her husband was the first one to notice the change. The difference was plain to see, a dragon swallowing the moon, a pattern from China that no one in Khouf had ever seen before. And Zahia had never set foot in China.

And then the guardian of the cemetery saw two stones,

chawaheds placed at the head and the foot of her grave. How did she do it? How could a dead woman unearth two stones sunk in the ground and move them? Abomination, cried the guardian of the cemetery.

For ten years, at night-time vigils, people have recounted the tale of Zahia. Noor speaks enviously of it, wants her own destiny to be fulfilled so that she too can enjoy the privilege reserved for the faithful. She'll come back to her house, she'll feed her goat and water her basil plant. But not her Barbary fig. It's mature enough to fend for itself.

You get up and prepare to leave but she tugs your sleeve and pulls you back. She has a question for you, the same one as before:

'Are you here to write a book? Why not write it about yourself? No one in Khouf knows you. What brings you to this village at the end of the world, when you could have set yourself up in a real house in a town, visited women who have cooking pots that shine like mirrors instead of pots coated with grime, women who have machines to do everything, to wash, iron, cook and even stitch shrouds?'

Conscious of having talked too much, she stops. She looks you up and down suspiciously. And then cuts you to the quick as she says:

'How do I know you're not a friend of the sheikh and the qadi? How do I know they're not paying you to get me to confess things to you?'

You suddenly realise that you don't know her name any

more than she knew the name of the cat carried off by the *khamsin*. 'Go and see the woman who is to be stoned,' Dr. Paul, the director of the Centre said to you. 'See if you can help her.'

'Noor', she whispers. 'My name is Noor.'

'Light', you translate, with your obsession for migrating words between your own native language and the French you learned at school. What you do not tell her is that you have not come here as an experienced aid worker, but because of a man. A man you loved, a man who was banished by his wife from his own home when she found out about your affair. And because of a cat, crushed beneath the wheels of a bin lorry. You went out to the garden that night, spade in hand, to dig a hole to bury the little ball of white fur, your tears flowing, an abandoned woman.

When he walked out and closed the door behind him, you put on the glasses he'd left on the bedside table, wondering what he saw when he looked at you. The girl reflected in the mirror was neither beautiful nor ugly, tall nor small, fat nor thin. Average in every respect. No reason to be spurned. And no reason to be admired either, you said to yourself as you turned the mirror to the wall.

Fear of being alone had led you to the International Aid Centre. You wanted to leave before winter and not see the rain soaking the little grave, not breathe in the smell of honey tobacco that suffused your sheets.

Volunteers were welcome, you would leave the following day.

For a small village on the edge of the desert, because your life too was a desert. To a region of famine, because you could swallow no food. To a drought-stricken land, because of your tears? Your task would be to convince the people that France Aide would protect them and save them from death by thirst and starvation.

With your plane ticket in hand, you were warned against getting involved in the people's private lives, against meddling in their tribal or religious customs.

When you arrived in Khouf after a day's journey by plane and bus, you vowed not to speak of your own troubles. But here you are, baring your soul to a woman who scarcely understands a word you are saying, a woman whose problems make yours pale in comparison. You tell her in detail of the pain you felt that night when you looked out of the window at the black void of your garden and saw the outline of your lover's lean figure through the glass, beckoning to you, the plump shape of the cat mewling to come inside. And of how you opened the window to let them in and were greeted only by wind and darkness.

You stand weeping before this woman who never sheds a tear, who wrings her hands in shame at her inability to console you. She does not look at you as she speaks, as the words line up in formation like toy soldiers and fall slowly from her dark brown lips.

She cannot believe that in your country, women spurn men, that a man can be banished from his own bed and thrown onto the street, that there is no outcry.

'Thank goodness!' she says, fervently pounding her chest with her fist. 'Foul, lazy fornicators they may be, but our men behave like men. They've always had the right to reject us, since the beginning of time. And to take us back if they choose to, if everything is done correctly. A spurned wife returns to her husband when she's fulfilled her duty to another man. "Under Ahmed first", the sheikh writes in his file, "then under Ali, then under Ahmed again." Problem solved. Yalalalalala! Married again, same as before.'

'What do you mean, "Under Ahmed", "under Ali"?'

Your question makes her laugh. A question only a *maboula* would ask. A fool, she adds in explanation, as though you were a child. The man is always on top, the woman underneath.

'He straddles her.'

'Never the other way round?' you venture.

'Never!'

Traditions must be respected. It is all written in the books. The creator of all things left nothing to chance: he created the mountains on high, the deserts below, the eagle in the air, the snake on the ground, the clouds in the sky, the mist over the land. The sheikh is the eye of Allah in the village, he has a list of forbidden acts; those who infringe the laws will be exposed on the great day of judgment.

As you stand up to go, she looks around her hut and her eye falls on a ladle hanging from a nail; she pulls it down and hands it to you. A gift, for you, a token of her friendship. You need it more than she does, she doesn't

17

cook any more, not since her husband stole her three sons from her. She pushes you out. Now that she has a friend in the *douar* she will do some housework. Everything must be left clean after she has gone, or the women will speak ill of her and her soul will suffer. Now she will sweep and water the floor of beaten earth, then she will pick up the broken branches in her garden, build a fire that will be visible across the desert, she will clean the cage, empty now that the chickens are gone and her husband has taken the rooster, she will milk the goat and give its milk to the poor. Noor wants nothing for herself. She cannot eat, she wants to keep nothing, leave nothing behind her.

Back at the Centre, your gaze sweeps over the low rooftops that seem to crawl along the ground, and Khouf appears to you to be trapped between mountain and desert. Khouf, a narrow ochre-coloured coffin. A snake of sand, its back cracked by drought. A snake sunk deep in torpor.

2.

At night, in your room furnished with a chair and a narrow bed, your thoughts turn to Noor waiting calmly to be stoned to death forty days from now. She would already have been executed if the earth, hardened by drought, hadn't been so resistant to the spade. An icy wind has been blowing all evening, stirring hopes of rain, but there are no clouds in its wake. The wind blows from all directions, bending palm trees to the ground, trampling the leafless branches of trees that bear no fruit. Trees as barren as you, who made no effort to protect yourself, knowing that a pregnancy would have forced your lover to leave his wife for you. Suddenly you want to touch him, to breathe in the smell of his skin. You scan the winding road that leads to the *douar*. He will appear any minute, you feel it in your belly. You press your stomach with both hands to still the spasms. Amina warned you to be wary of this swirling wind that arouses the flesh and makes a lonely woman believe a man, heavy with desire, is about to knock on her door. This wind is so like the *khamsin*, only its fire is replaced by ice. Cruel and bounteous, capable of extremes, the best and the worst, this wind can blow for three or thirty days. The wind on four wheels, the camel drivers call it. A hammer brandished by a giant, it knocks the tops off mountains, taking years off the rocks, ageing the plains and women alike.

When your lover walked out with his bags and you realised you wouldn't see him again, you suddenly felt old. Old and full of rage, ready to bite the door he closed behind him, sink your teeth into the clods of earth turned up by your spade as you dug a grave amid the sage and the jasmine. A man and a cat, taking turns to share your bed for a year. When the man wasn't there, the cat would claim his place and set in motion his purring machine, a sound like the gurgling of a hookah issuing from his little muzzle. You would dream of ottoman palaces, of a sultan whose favourite you were.

'You're only interested in things that don't last,' a friend said accusingly one day. 'Married men, thoroughbred cats. Next time, go for a mongrel.' Man or cat, she didn't say.

When the hole was filled with earth, you fled, not wanting to look your problem in the face. You preferred to let time do its work.

Nursing your own wounds, you can do nothing for Noor, or for the people of Khouf. After one morning in the Centre, you realised you were as bereft as the people you had come to help. Old Jalila told you she wanted wheat flour, not the maize flour she can't digest, and you turned your back on her. You turned a deaf ear to the rantings of a giant with three wives and twelve children demanding three times his share of flour, sugar and rice.

You admire Dr. Paul's patience, as he runs the Centre, takes care of the sick and listens calmly to the recriminations of the dissatisfied. Before he came here, he was a doctor in a small town. He could have slipped comfortably into retirement, but he chose to come to Khouf. A good man in a God-forsaken land. His short-sighted eyes light up when they see a child, any child. Scrawny and dirty, bellies swollen, enlarged heads on skeletal frames, Dr. Paul finds beauty in all of them. He examines them, ruffles their unwashed hair, makes them swallow a few drops of liquid before he gives them a biscuit, a square of chocolate, or sometimes, a piece of meat when a local peasant has sold his cow. The mothers call him "*Hakim*", wise man. The children sit with their backs against the wall, their spindly limbs unable to support them, staring at him with weary, unblinking eyes. Their gaze takes in the landscape where no birds fly, even the crickets have fled, a landscape of stony ground dotted with thistles, where only reptiles can find sustenance.

Whatever you do, you cannot escape your own sorrows. The suffering of the people of Khouf only reminds you of your lover's departure, the death of your cat. Your petty griefs have shrunk your heart. You are not ready to give, even less to receive. You turn away when a mother thanks you. You pull your hand away when a man tries to kiss it.

The bags of sugar, rice and flour you distribute do not come from you. You reject everything utterly, people and places. You avoid walking by the cemetery with its tombs sunk into the sand. The stones facing Mecca remind you of the hole dug by your hand in your garden.

When a couple comes into the Centre, side by side, or even with the woman behind the man, you think of the couple you failed to become and feel as if you have been slapped in the face. Eight hours in a plane, another eight hours in a bus, and all to find yourself able to speak only to a woman condemned to death by stoning at the hands of her own people. Your petty troubles seem laughable beside such desolation. You jump at any chance to leave the office and run to her house, leaving Amina, who can barely read and write, to divide up parcels and record names.

You suspect people of lying, think they are lazy, lacking in imagination. Why don't they plant alfalfa, you ask yourself, instead of the maize that demands so much water? Marry one woman instead of two or three, when they can barely feed one wife? Have two children instead of eight? Tend a small vegetable plot instead of these tracts that stretch out into the desert and become gaping sores, cankers delivered up to the thistles, desert upon desert?

A few hours were enough for you to understand that you will be of no help at all to these people. When you were asked to go and see the woman condemned to death by stoning, you were quick to take the narrow path to her house, resolved to stay away from the Centre until the people in need had all left.

3.

Amina brandishes an envelope with a French stamp. She's been watching out for your return.

'A letter for you!' she shouts. 'From your lover. It's heavy, must be a marriage proposal.'

She expects to see you jumping for joy, not with this pained, closed expression on your face.

'Have you been to see the stoned woman?'

Realising her tongue has betrayed her thoughts, she adds:

'The woman condemned to stoning? Take my advice: leave her to her fate. It's not the first time a sinful woman has been put to death. There are thousands like her. Just ask the gravestones.'

She stuffs the envelope into your bra as if it were a mailbox. She'd give anything to know what the letter says.

Your silence infuriates her.

'So, when's the wedding day?' she asks. 'I'll have to get myself a new dress.'

It's probably a letter to say it's all over, you tell her.

Thinking it will make you feel better, she tells you that her cousin's husband repudiated her three times in ten years of marriage, but every time, he took her back.

'Under Mohammed first and then under Hassan', you recite, just as Noor had done scarcely an hour earlier.

'Listen to you, foreign woman,' Amina says, 'talking just like us. Next thing you know, you'll be wearing the *hijab*.'

"You left me to face the music alone," your lover complains. "Going back home to my wife didn't calm her down at all. She's demanding a divorce; she's turned the children against me. Our friends are taking sides; they're saying I was having an affair with you. When we divide up our assets, their word will matter. You can help me by writing a letter to my wife. Tell her you're just an old friend, that there was never anything serious between us. Do this for me, in the name of our love."

You swallow your bile. Better the cruelty of Noor's husband than this whining cowardice. Sensing your sadness, Amina makes no more effort to find out what is in the letter. She gives you a glass of rose water, makes sure you gulp it all down. It feels like a drop of rain on sun-baked stone. Instantly evaporated.

'Cry,' she tells you, walking around you as if to encircle your pain. 'Cry! To hell with the drought!' She swells with pride to see you laughing through the tears. You've done as she said, the sun has come out, she's shown you the rainbow.

'Yalalalalala.'

Excitement bubbles all around you. A film is to be screened in the square this evening. A gift from the people of France. You wonder if the white sheet strung between two palm trees will withstand the sand-laden wind. And Gonzagues, the young medical student and makeshift projectionist, will he know which way to thread the film? And then there's the film itself, donated by the Red Cross. The crowd has been gathering on the square since noon, all jostling to get a place in the front row, women elbowing each other out of the way, men using their fists. What will they make of the film?

Everyone waits for the sheikh to arrive. The film can't begin until he's given it his blessing. All eyes are turned towards the village's only road. The projectionist makes a few test runs and seems satisfied. Then the drums announce the sheikh's arrival. Adults and children bow down as he passes. You are the only one to turn your back on him, your eyes searching in the darkness for Noor's small house. The glimmer of light between two cactus leaves comes from her lamp. The sound of the drums must be a reminder to her of the sentence that awaits her, of the executioners who will come to her house and call to her through the hedge to come out. It is she who must go out to them, for the faithful are forbidden to cross the threshold of an adulterous woman.

Everyone stares at the screen, rumpled now by the wind. The carpet laid out on the ground is reserved for the sheikh, the qadi and the mayor. No such privileges for the muezzin: repeating the words of the Prophet doesn't make him important. Might as well honour a parrot. Gonzagues claps his hands and the chatter turns to whispers. The only sound is the hum of the generator, brought here on a donkey's back, purring like a huge cat. The crowd is expecting to see pictures on the screen, but first they hear only music: the Marseillaise rings out. The projectionist should have cut it, but no one seems concerned. The crowd prostrate themselves, foreheads to the ground, in response to what must surely be a French muezzin proclaiming the greatness of Allah.

They sit upright again, listening intently as a half-naked blond appears on the screen.

'A queen', the women exclaim in admiration as they chew their qat.

'A young bride', the young women say, disagreeing and throwing their heads back to ululate to the stars.

'A whore,' the men complain.

With her unveiled face and that low-cut dress, she must be a whore. Hostile shouts erupt when the queen, the young bride, the whore throws down a ring given to her by a fat man with a moustache. She slaps him and people start to push and shove. Women and children search for the ring in the sand. Their husbands pull the screen down, trampling on it with both feet.

Daggers are drawn. The tension is palpable. Now that the screen has gone and with it the brazen woman, the men turn on Gonzagues. This is his doing, he must be made to pay the price, for the unveiled woman, for the lost ring, for the humiliated suitor. A man who loses his honour becomes female, says the proverb. Neither man nor woman. His organ shrivels like dried paper, shrinks to nothing, he becomes a creature apart, there's no place for him either in heaven or hell.

The sheikh tries to restore order. He hits out at random, but no one pays attention.

In the confusion, you slip away.

Sitting in her doorway, Noor asks you to tell her about the film. She caught some of the sounds. You tell her about the woman, the ring, the slap.

'You expect me to believe she slapped her husband?'

'He's not necessarily her husband, but she did slap him.'

'It's a wonder he didn't kill her!' she exclaims.

'Maybe he did, but we'll never know now. After the slap, that was it for the film. The men went for the projectionist. The sheikh left, with his stick, and the children are still looking for the diamond.'

She yawns widely.

'Zahi will find it. My son has the eyes of a lynx.'

You try not to laugh, not wanting to offend her.

She says she quite enjoyed it. She liked the music. She even danced a bit even though she'd always believed she couldn't dance.

'Whirling around like a top, I was, tapping my feet, I felt like I was flying.'

What metal is she made of, this woman who is forbidden to see her children but is content to launder their clothes? To dance to the sound of the drums from the village entertainment she is forbidden to attend? Excluded from village life, Noor can only measure her days by the appearance of the muezzin, the diminutive figure suspended between earth and sky, his call echoing over the desert five times a day. He is her speaking clock, her calendar. She says she is not to be pitied, that she is not as alone as you think. Women from the village come right up to her hedge, place plates there, left-overs from meals, sheets.

'You can wash them for us', they shout, their faces hidden by their veils. 'It'll help you pass the time.'

She talks to you about her husband, Moha. In the darkness, she feels free to speak frankly, to tell you that beneath the fearless, swaggering exterior lurks an idle, cowardly liar. It was when a dog attacked her that she saw him in his true colours. It happened one night when they were on their way home from a wedding. The dog went for her, it was ready to eat her alive. Terrified, she screamed and called out to Moha to help.

'Stop calling my name,' he hissed, cowering behind a low wall. 'You'll lead it straight to where I am.'

The dog decided it wasn't interested in Noor and ran off. Moha emerged from his hiding place brandishing a stick, waving it around and whipping up the sand, threatening to reduce the vanished dog to a pulp if it ever dared go near his wife again.

Noor shrieks with laughter, crying and laughing at the same time. At the sound of her laughter, the goat appears and Noor grabs it by the legs, ties them up and holds the animal out to you.

'She'd be happier in your house, foreign woman. She's been so sad since she heard about the fatwa.'

You tell her the goat would get in your way, that it needs a garden, but Noor brushes aside your objections with her hand.

'Hide her in your cupboard or under your bed. Or else slit her throat and make a stew of her, bones and all. A feast for your Frenchies, the ones who think they can bring us rain just by coming here.'

4.

I, Amina, nobody's daughter, intend to find out who she is, this foreign woman. She's out, gone to see Noor as usual, and I've grabbed the chance to search through her things. Two skirts, two blouses, two books and a photo of a cat. She can't have come from too far away if that's all she needs. Maybe she just came over the mountains and they spat her out in front of the aid workers' door. Or perhaps she's only here for Noor, to keep her company and taunt the sheikh and the qadi. She's not interested in anyone else. Doesn't look twice at the sick and the hungry, ignores the scroungers who get their kicks from begging. No, I think she's only here for Noor. Those eyes of hers, the mukhtar says they aren't real. They're made of glass, you can see the sky through them, that's why they're blue. She's so full of herself, I can't for the life of me see why. She does know a thing or two though, I'll give her that. A mine of information, speaks three languages no less, she can read and write them too. Unheard of in Khouf, where the only school is a madrasa that doubles as a grain store in the harvest season. Unheard of even in the Sahel, where they have real schools. Three languages and she doesn't even know how to hold a broom properly or wring out a mop with a single squeeze. She's a woman on several levels, like the houses in the city. Upstairs for the breeze to blow through, a middle floor for hiding from prying eyes, and downstairs for visitors. When I'd finished going through her bags I had just one question: are they so short of children in Paris – where she claims to be from – that she has to adopt a cat that weighs barely a kilo? A cat? Why didn't she adopt an orphan from Khouf? It's not as if there aren't plenty of them here.

As soon as she got here, she took out the photo of the creature and showed it to Dr. Paul. Quite overcome, he was, said his daughter had a cat just like it. Same colour. And I thought only people came in different colours. I tried to explain to her that a cat is just a cat. It's not a child from someone's family, a kid with vagrants for parents. The cats in Khouf are all the same colour, neither black nor white, they're all grey like the mountain, like the sky that's managed not to rain for the past two years, holding back its tears. But she acted like she didn't hear. Why on earth she showed her cat to Dr. Paul I don't know. I mean she could have shown it to Gonzagues. Now there's a man who could make the sun move out of his way, but she doesn't like him. She's only interested in old men, womanisers who aren't to be trusted. That doctor is as old as the hills. His actual age is a mystery. And as for family, who knows? His patients are his children, the sick people he examines, licking his lips as if he was chewing on halva. He'll keep on poking and prodding and looking after them until his hands drop off and his voice makes a noise like a twisted spoon scraping a bowl. The foreign woman's done something to him. Why else would he let her spend all her time with Noor? Noor, who doesn't need any help now that her sons have left her and she's got nothing to do.

He's a good man, that doctor. He's good like the medicine man who cures the blind, pure as the water of Zamzam that washes away all our sins. He's thoughtful too, he lifts his feet off the floor when I'm mopping. Not like Gonzagues, who just walks all over it. He likes to see me on all fours, Gonzagues, arse in the air like a mare ready to be mounted. It's not as if there aren't plenty of goats in Khouf for him to relieve himself with, plenty of holes in walls too, and tree trunks. Why ask me to put my head up my arse? I've heard that putting your head down lower than your hindquarters like that makes your brains spill out. I don't know who it was, someone I don't know, who said it to someone else, who told me. If I'd been born somewhere different, I'd be rich. I'd be able to take care of myself. But here I am in the worst place in the world. I'd be a gleaming fish if I'd been born in some other place, I'd be white on the outside and pink on the inside like Gonzagues' girlfriend, a houri the colour of Turkish delight.

He'd have to turn her photo to the wall when he manhandles me, instead of staring into the whites of her eyes and burbling "Aline, Aline" with every shove. Aline, like Ali. And there I was wondering if Gonzagues was Shia, saying the name of the Prophet's son-in-law with such fervour. Ali, father of two martyrs: Hasan and Hussein. Those two definitely made it into Allah's great paradise.

Ali, Hasan, Hussein. Gonzagues doesn't even know who they are.

He does know about Muhammad though. He calls him Mahomet, three syllables repeated five times a day, he says, called out by the muezzin braying louder than the donkey in the brickworks.

He can't wait to get back home, Gonzagues. Not like the foreign woman who wouldn't care if she never sets foot there again. I mean, Paris it may be, but there's just as much hate there, they still kill each other. Maybe she killed someone back there in Paris. To hate, you have to know how to love, the proverb says. She's not capable of passion, the foreign woman. She's eaten up with pity for Noor, she's just a bleeding heart.

Murderer or not, she shows me respect. Not like Gonzagues. When he's done riding me, if he doesn't spit on me he takes it out on the furniture, laying into the desk and the chair, putting the boot in. Weird how he makes me turn my back on him while he's doing his business, as if we were mad at each other.

'Can I ask you a question?' I said to the foreign woman this morning before she went off to Noor's. She was dividing up beans, flour, sugar and rice into packets and she thought a bit and said: 'I'll answer you if I can.'

'In Paris, do they have sex like chickens, from behind? Or do they do it like whores, face to face?'

I thought she was going to hit me. Her hands were busy tying up the bags, then she pulled a face, and that spurred me on to ask another question even though I know the answer. I just wanted to keep on talking to her, to feel like I have a friend.

'And the trees, foreign woman, how do they make babies? Ever seen palm trees climbing on top of each other?'

She tried not to laugh and drilled her finger into her temple to show she thought I was crazy.

Noor, who knows all about these things, once said to me: 'Of course trees get on top of each other.' She must know what she's talking about. After all, she's been had, at least four times. Given birth to three ingrates, and a fourth one to come, if they let her stay alive long enough to drop it. 'They do it at night when men are asleep, when the khamsin is blowing and no one is looking outside.'

It's always the khamsin with Noor. She can't imagine love without it.

5.

All morning, there's been a smell of rain in the air. The sky holds back, taunting the people of Khouf. They stare up at the clouds, making out here and there the shape of a rabbit, a sheep, a one-eyed cow.

'Cold and drought are the legs of Satan,' goes the saying.

You too gaze up at the clouds, scanning the sky through your open window. A face looms above the windowsill: it's Amina, signalling to you to join her outside. She has a surprise for you.

A surprise? Does she mean the figure at her side, swathed in black?

Noor. You recognise her eyes of blue-green water. She shouldn't be here; she's not supposed to go out at all. This is Amina's doing, her idea to disguise the sinner as a Salem witch. Delighted to see your shocked reaction they giggle, stifling their laughter with their hands. Amina says they're just paying a visit to the well of the most benevolent of saints, Sitt Zainab, the only one who can transform the girl child in a woman's belly into a boy. And Noor will give anything for this child to be a *weled*, a boy. There's no need to worry, they'll be back soon.

You remind Noor that barely a month ago she wanted to be rid of the child, that she already has three ungrateful, cold-hearted sons who have forgotten her. But she stops you with a wave of her hand.

'How do you know the fourth one won't be the best of all?' Noor, full of maternal pride, boasts of having given birth only to sons. 'And the other three,' she crows, 'cold-hearted and ungrateful or not, they are *weleds*.'

'What if Moha discovers you've been out, or the sheikh?'

'That one-eyed sheikh? He only sees half of what goes on. And Moha has too much on his plate these days to notice anything. He hasn't got time to watch over his wife, he has his casino to think about. A good thing it is too. At long last he'll make a bit of money, after all these years of squandering it.'

You try to imagine a casino, here on the edge of the desert, like in Las Vegas. Wondering what else you can say to persuade them not to go, you warn them they could get caught in a downpour, that the well could be dry.

Just going there is enough, they retort indignantly.

Amina points out that they haven't come to ask you for advice. It's help they want. You're the only one who can take them to the well. Dr. Paul will be only too happy to let you use his car. If someone doesn't drive it somewhere soon, it'll end up being used as a chicken coop.

'But I can't drive.'

'Maybe not in Paris,' they say, 'but here in the desert you can. A donkey could drive a car here.'

As far as they're concerned, driving a car is simply a matter of turning the key and putting your foot down. The car will drive itself, the Prophet himself won't be able to stop it.

'All the way to China,' Noor adds.

You look perturbed and Amina tells you not to worry, a car is little sister to the donkey, the mule's cousin. Paved roads, dirt tracks, it knows all them all. Let it know you trust it and it will go back to its garage by itself, like a horse going back to its stable.

You shake your head, turn away from them, still shaking your head. They're exhausting.

Amina pulls herself up to her full height and throws her disappointment in your face. She was wrong about you. She thought you cared. In the end, you're just like all the others who come from "over there", all head and no heart. She tells you to let Dr. Paul know that she's not coming in today. She's taking a day off, accompanying a pregnant woman on a pilgrimage, doing her duty as a good Muslim should.

Your two friends are as unpredictable as the *khamsin*, the wind that blows when you least expect it. Scarcely a month ago, Noor was ready to give herself an abortion with a knitting needle. Amina was accusing her of every sin and depravity in the world. And now here they are singing each other's praises and extolling Moha's virtues. No longer the terrible father, the eternal loser, now he is an astute businessman, a good match. So good that all the girls in Khouf dream of marrying him. Hurling their parting words at you, Noor and Amina turn on their heels and walk away without a backward glance, their robes sweeping the ground behind them.

You watch them as they head for the desert, gesticulating as they walk. They disappear into the distance, Amina supporting Noor, Noor leaning on Amina. As you close the window they are no more than two black dots in the expanse of ochre.

You go and join your colleagues in the Centre, give them the list of people who have received food aid: Mohammed, Hammoudi, Ahmed, Hassan, Hussein, Hussoun. One name stands out, Robert. A Frenchman, in need of food aid? You ask the person in charge, then the aid workers. They say that Mr. Robert is an engineer, in charge of the construction of the dam fifty kilometres upstream. He comes every Saturday, usually in the evening, to take delivery of the sacks of flour, rice and sugar for the workers' canteen.

He comes from the other side of the mountain, they say, in a jeep, the only one in the region.

You feel light-headed as Noor's words come back to you: 'He was a foreigner. I could tell from the smell of him. Our men smell of burnt sand, quenched fire. All those years digging in the phosphorus mines. That's all gone now, the mining company's gone back to America. But the smell stayed here, on the men, the sulphur working its way under their skin, clinging to their bodies. Everything, sweat, piss, blood, it all smells of flared matches. No, he was a foreigner. And the jeep. No man from around here can afford one of those.'

Noor had pointed out the site of the old mine, the gash on the side of the mountain with its maze of underground passages, where Satan gave the orders, or so she'd heard. It was Satan who told the men where to dig, decided who should drill, carry, man the conveyor belt. Satan who gave the order to stop work when a mineshaft collapsed.

You remember thinking that Noor saw the devil's work everywhere.

The sound of an engine wrenches you from your thoughts. A jeep pulls up in a cloud of dust, outside the warehouse entrance. A man emerges, handsome, fiftyish, well-dressed, a tailored tweed jacket, eyes of the same silvery-blue as his hair. You rush down the corridor that leads to the warehouse, ready to confront this man, to shout at him that a local woman might die because of him, that he raped her while she was out looking for her cat, that it is his duty to turn himself in.

By the time you reach the end of the corridor, he has already gone. You swallow your words as you see the car driving off at high speed, as if pursued by all the devils in hell. His lordship the engineer only needed two minutes to collect the sacks of food earmarked for him.

'Hey!' you bellow at him, 'Robert!' as if you've known each other for years. 'Stop!'

Your shouts continue to ring out, while the dust settles and dusk takes possession of the landscape.

6.

One by one, the lights come on in Khouf. Only Noor's remains unlit. The rain, the first for months, is greeted with ululations and muffled drumbeats. The downpour should have driven Noor and Amina back to the village. You stay up late into the night, the only person watching for their return, consumed by thoughts of chasms waiting to swallow them up, of famished wolves ready to raid the villages at the first sign of winter. Gonzagues, Dr. Paul's young assistant, reassures you with his customary cynicism, telling you that human beings don't just evaporate like puddles in the sun, that people are always found in the end, even if it's only their bones.

You feel like slapping him. Amina was right to call westerners heartless. Just as you are preparing for bed, you see a tiny glimmer of light between two leaves of Noor's Barbary fig. You run, splashing through puddles, inhaling deeply the pepper and salt smell of the wet palms. When you reach the hedge, you call out to her and rush headlong into the house. Inside, the house is suffused with cold and damp. The only sign of Noor is a foot sticking out from under a blanket. You crouch down beside the mattress and talk to her about the man in the jeep, tell her you know where to find him, but all she can think of is her impending death. She wants another blanket, wants you stop up the holes in the walls with stones, wants you to immure her alive.

You search around for a blanket and find only an old carpet, one of the few items that Moha did not take. Noor is bathed in sweat. She complains that she is cold, begs you to listen to her. You struggle to understand her words. She says there's no cause for celebration, the man in the jeep must have washed more than a hundred times since he "mounted" her. Any sign that he was in her belly will have vanished. She tells you to forget about it, not to think of it as rape, perhaps he loved her, if not she would have called out, alerted the whole village. Noor wants you to think only of the child, to adopt the baby after her death. Whatever happens, she wants you to hide the child from Moha, he'd think nothing of drowning it, just like the cats she used to bring home.

'Take the baby, foreign woman. Say he came from your own womb. Take him to your country, make him French like you, like Dr. Paul.'

You tell her there will be no baby if she dies now, that her baby will perish with her, but she continues to insist that she wants you to take him.

43

Squatting on the cold ground, you massage her shoulders, her feet. You make her swallow two aspirin and then light the fire in the hearth with the last remaining log.

She kisses your hands ardently, tells you she's ashamed of herself, she should have listened to you. Amina had planned it all, without asking her. She shouldn't have gone along with her. Sitt Zainab wasn't in her well, it was all dried up. She must have gone to another well.

Exhausted, Noor pulls the carpet up around her. The baby will be a boy, she announces.

'A *weled*, foreign woman, Sitt Zainab heard my prayers.'

7.

'Are you the one making Noor believe she's going to have a boy?' you ask Amina.

'Allah preserve me from such a thing! Who am I to make assumptions about what the Creator has in store? It was the stone that spoke. One stone among all the others at Sitt Zainab's well. Noor raised the stone and saw a lizard. She'd have seen ants if she was carrying a girl.'

'Did you know she's not well, not well at all?'

'She'll get over it', Amina retorts harshly.

'She was coughing all night, she couldn't breathe. I'm going to ask Dr Paul to go and see her.'

'You want her to take off her clothes in front of a man?' she counters, turning her back on you. 'A man she doesn't even know?'

You make her turn round and look you in the eye, you shake her, accuse her of having dragged Noor off on a foolish escapade, of making her ill. She lets you shake her, makes no attempt to break free, stands motionless in the face of your anger. Huge tears, as big as pigeon's eggs, roll down her cheeks. She throws herself at you, as if to pummel you with her fists, and clasps you in her arms. Together, you weep, held in each other's embrace.

'*Okhti*, you are my *okhti*,' she sobs. 'My sister,' you say, echoing her words.

Dr. Paul, who has been watching your exchange, is taken aback by this sudden change of mood. 'You should save your tears for the corn shrivelling in the fields day after day,' he says, handing you a bag of medicines: tablets to bring down the fever, antibiotics, a bottle of cough syrup, two bananas.

Outside it is still dark. You go straight to Noor's house, not waiting for the sun to come up. Fear clutches at your belly as you make your way through the village. The night has never seemed so black, walls close in on you as you walk through the streets. Dogs bark at you, aroused by the unmistakable smell of a stranger. The square still looks like a battle-ground, the screen lying where it fell, coated in mud. No one has picked up the pieces of the shattered projector.

Amina has taken a short cut and is waiting for you at Noor's house. She can't find Noor, she tells you as you draw near. She's not on her mattress, she's not curled up by the hearth in front of the fire. She's been abducted, someone has taken her and killed her, to make it clear to you she can't be saved from the fatwa, that your efforts are futile. You hear a dry cough coming from the lean-to next to the house, and find Noor, huddled next to the goat for warmth, lying in a bed she's made up for herself. She says she'll go back to her house when it is not so cold. She's moved to her secondary residence, her self-satisfied look seems to say. You sponge her down and change her sheets while Amina prepares some herbal tea, tossing a handful of leaves into boiling water as she utters invocations to Satan, *ta'wizat* to coax him from Noor's body. No mention of Allah, only Satan.

Noor sleeps. You and Amina speak in hushed voices to avoid waking her. Amina thinks you should go back to the city, talk to the people in power. Only the rulers of the Republic can save Noor.

'Forget about the sheikh and the qadi. Forget about Moha, he carries no more weight than a grasshopper's wing. No one will listen to you here. You're a woman, a Christian, you make new enemies in the village every day. The men are accusing you of turning their wives away from the Sharia. Your uncovered head is a provocation – hair on your head, hair between your legs, it's all the same. They suspect you of using Noor to solve your own problems. They say you were spurned by a man, fated to be humiliated. You're using Noor as your weapon against your own destiny. Why else would you have travelled across land and sea to bury yourself here in this village forgotten by Allah and all his prophets?'

Amina warns you against everyone and everything you have come into contact with here, even the palm trees. The men of Khouf are as silent as the desert, as unyielding as the mines that no longer respond to the blows from their shovels.

Turn around, go to the city. Tell them there you are a foreign journalist and doors will open for you. Ask for an audience with the Minister for the Prevention of Vice, with the mullah responsible for the protection of virtue. Tell them the west is watching them. The sheikh's fatwa will be swept away, erased like camel dung in the desert. Go tomorrow. There's one bus, Abdul's. It will take you across the desert all the way to the city. It's always on time. Five hours on the road and you'll be in another world, in the twentieth century. Buses, bikes, trains, and not a donkey in sight, no mules either. Go straight to the Home for Widows and Orphans. The women who run it have arms as long as the branches of the medlar tree. They know all the important people.

8.

Noor doubts that a mullah or a minister would be interested in her case. As far as they are concerned she does not exist. They don't know her, they've never met her, never seen a photograph of her. She's never had her picture taken. She doesn't even have an identity card.

'These people are important, like champion football players, especially the mullah. He made his pilgrimage to Mecca on foot. My death will weigh no more than three beans. They don't grant pardons lightly. Much better not to ask for too much. Ask them to delay stoning me, put it off until after the birth of my child. My baby's done nothing wrong. He wants to live, he's clinging to life with all his might. The knitting needle did nothing to him. It just made me bleed a little, no more than a thimble-full.'

She casts her gaze around her simple dwelling. Her hand lights on the only piece of furniture she possesses – a trunk of some kind. She raises the lid and takes out a silk shawl, gives it a shake and places it round your shoulders.

Her bridal shawl, she wore it once, on the day of her wedding. You can wear it in town, where women dress in finery. Seeing you hesitate, she explains that it was a gift from Moha's father. She was supposed to marry him. He changed his mind at the last minute and gave her to his son, Moha, the man who loves raki and gambling, and now his niece, but that's another story.

'Why didn't he give you to his uncle?' you ask, your voice shaking with anger. 'Or why not his grandfather?'

'Moha was the only one who'd have me, drunkard that he is. The state he was in, he'd have married anything. A girl without a dowry is like a garden without flowers. I had nothing to my name but the dress I stood up in.'

She walks around you, admiring you in her shawl as if she were looking at herself in the mirror. Fleeting as a ray of sun between two clouds, her light mood is soon gone. Worry darkens her small bony face again, filling her blue-green eyes.

She asks how you plan to go about getting her stoning delayed.

'I'll tell them you were raped. That the stranger forced you. You cried out but no one heard you over the *kham-sin*. You struggled but he overpowered you, crushed you beneath him, tore your clothes.'

Her eyes blacken with rage.

'Why tell a lie? Does it change anything if you tell them I gave my consent? A rapist takes what he wants and runs off like a thief in the night. The man who took me kept starting again, three times. I was just what he wanted. He must have found me to his taste, as delicious as lamb cooked in its own juices, as corn-fed chicken, as…"

She runs out of examples, choked with anger, unable to continue her litany. Metaphors fail her and she bursts into tears.

She tells you between sobs that the man had been gentle with her. Tender and attentive to her desires, generous with his caresses. He had probed her with his sex, with his fingers, she was full to the brim. Her belly became a lake, a river. To say he had taken her only once is worse than a lie, a slap in the face. The women of the village will laugh at her, malicious gossips will spread rumours. They will say her sex is rough and hairy, as rough as the coat of a donkey beaten by its master.

9.

Odd, the foreign woman, burying herself in this hole that even grasshoppers don't look twice at. They fly over here with their eyes closed, it's so ugly. So she lost her lover and a cat. Is that enough to make her want to fall this low? Down here at the end of the world? All she'd have to do is hang a bit of wool from her belt to a tree outside the zawiya and she'd have a man throwing himself at her feet soon enough. And a cat. A man much less married than the other one too, and a cat not so ready to die. But she's one of those people who has to have everything right now. She came to Khouf to punish herself. We're the sticks she's beating herself with. She's filling her life with crumbs from other people's lives, Noor's most of all. She can't wait to get through her work at the Centre and go rushing off towards Noor's Barbary fig and tell her that no one will touch a hair on her head so long as she's alive. And when I said something about going to talk to the minister and the mullah, she took me at my word. I was just talking to hear the sound of my own voice, but she's decided to take herself off to the city to plead with the bigwigs. They don't care about Noor, they've never heard of her. No one has outside of this village. No one cares about us, with our two-wheeled carts and our donkeys swaying around like drunkards. If you've got cars with four wheels, trams that glide straight along on rails, why would you care about Noor? The stones piled up in the square will get what they want, Noor will be stoned. Like the white flowers of aoussaj that bloom in the desert after the first rain, she'll have had her time. The next day, they're gone, vanished without trace, not even a wilted petal remains. That's how Noor will end up, like assouaj in the desert.

Old Jalila says aoussaj is nothing but a mirage. She thinks she knows everything, but she doesn't even know from one day to the next what stone she'll lay her head on at night. When Noor's dead, the walls of her house will crumble away from neglect. All that will be left of her will be the rags torn from her dress, hanging on her hedge.

She'll still call out to Zahi, Zein, Zad when she's dead and buried three metres under ground. She'll call to them to come and eat the meal she won't have prepared for lack of arms to cook the rice and breath to blow life into the flame beneath the pot.

Yesterday she asked me to bring her three locks of their hair so she could put them with her ta'wiza, the charms she wears around her neck. Dr. Paul has declared war on head lice and told the barber to shave all the children's heads, so all I'd have to do is pick it up and Allah would reward me in the next world. It all went according to plan, except for the mothers who wanted to do it their own way, with their child's head in their laps. They pick out the creatures, squash them between their thumb and index finger and throw them away for the dogs to snap up as they go by. The doctor saw me filching the bits of hair and winked at me knowingly. He has a pendant round his neck with a lock of blond hair. Twenty-five years wasted over the body of a little girl spat out by the sea. He still thinks of how she might have emerged from the waves and walked through the door of the house by the sea to get on with her life. He couldn't stand living by the sea that killed his child any longer. He left his village in Brittany and signed up to do humanitarian work somewhere inland, in a drought-stricken place. Water will always make him think of the drenched yellow dress, the dress that looked from a distance like a ray of sun refracted by the windows. He's old but he's put off retiring, he can't face going back to the house by the sea where his wife is waiting for him. "I'll come back when I feel strong enough to face up to the sea", he wrote to her a little while ago. But time's passing and he's not getting any stronger. He's decided to be sensible, he says. He's going to wall up the side of the house that's open onto the sea, put the door on the other side. Turn his back on the horizon.

She's throwing herself into the lion's den, the foreign woman, appearing before the minister and the mullah, talking to them as if they were part of her world. And when she's done with the two bigwigs of the Republic, no doubt she'll go and knock on Allah's door and ask him to save Noor from stoning.

Sometimes I think she's more interested in Noor's child than in Noor herself. It's the egg she wants, not the chicken. Once the baby's hatched and Noor's buried under the stones, she'll carry it off under her arm. Goodbye Khouf. No one's going to stop her taking a sinner's child off to the land of sinners.

Noor's baby will speak French, eat pork, like the French. If it's a girl, she'll leave her hair uncovered, show her ears. The foreign woman will say she brought the baby into the world all by herself, without the help of a man, like Sitt Miriam, mother of Isa, two thousand years ago. Let her take it, good riddance to it. The world will go on turning. Some little kid isn't going to change anything. The mullah will still buy his new babouches, the minister will still repudiate his wife and replace her with wife number four. "Four wives, if you treat them with fairness", the Qu'ran says. A fourth wife, younger, not ruined by pregnancies. I dreamt yesterday that the stones piled up in the square all flew away, like birds migrating, heading for the Sahel and the sea. But it was only a dream. The stones are still there. More have been added to the pile, bigger ones, heavy enough to split your head open in one blow. I cried without knowing why, then I dried my tears and told myself that dreams never saved anyone, any more than reading and writing did, and no book learning is going to make a real mother of the foreign woman. How's she going to feed it, with breasts dry as gourds left out in the sun?

What did she know of Khouf before she set foot here? What did she know of the earth reddened from the blood of the khamsin? Nothing. Why else would she have come with an umbrella? Can you imagine such a thing, in this village where the clouds just pass by with their legs crossed so they can go and piss somewhere else? There it was, forgotten in some corner of the Centre, only to end up on a rubbish heap near Jalila's place. The old woman thought it was a hat and paraded around the douar with it from one end to the other, convinced she was making quite an impression.

To hear me talk, you'd think I don't appreciate the foreign woman, that I don't have any respect for her, but you'd be wrong. I'd give anything to be like her: crossing my legs, smoking cigarettes, showing my hair and my toes, especially the toes, plump and white. Me with my dark, bony face. Toes shining like candles in the dark.

Yes, I'd give my right hand to be the foreign woman, to have a different life, not to be ashamed any more of being born a woman with an extra hole for men and their needs, for men to spill their juice into, the way they spit and vomit, of being a glove for their middle finger, a case for their ney, when they don't even know how to play the ney and when music is just a noise for them, a noise like any other.

She's some kind of official, the foreign woman, according to Gonzagues, and he is too, and Dr. Paul and all of the Frenchies. They all know how to read and write, she says so herself. How can you tell her that in Khouf the madrasa only accepts boys, that they learn to read the Qu'ran there, to write a few sentences, while the girls stay at home, reading minds and making good-luck or bad-luck charms to order: charms to bring back a straying husband, charms to cast a spell on a rival, to infect her with a deadly disease, disfigure her without raising a finger to her, harm her gently, as if knocking on a half-open door with compassion in your heart. To spill her blood as you spill the water for ablutions, reciting the prayer known to all believers worthy of being called so.

The foreign woman is my waking dream, a dream that walks, eats and sleeps. She is all that it is impossible for me to be. My skin is covered in goose-bumps when she writes. It's as if she were scratching me. That's what she says when I ask her what she's doing. She says she's scratching the paper.

You're definitely better off being born in the north. Abdul says the sun turns your brains to mush in the south. So Khouf must be further south than anywhere else in the world, right?

10.

Dawn breaks red in Khouf. The sun's first rays touch the mountains, suffusing them with the colour of the sulphur once mined in them. You hear three light knocks on your door, like a woodpecker tapping on the bark of a tree. It's Amina. She tells you she was woken by the sun. She's decided to go with you to the bus stop to persuade you to go to the Home for Widows and Orphans as soon as you arrive in the city. 'It's in the centre of the city,' she says, '*Beyt al armala wal yatim*, it's in the main square. The women there would walk through fire to help their sisters.' You remind her that Noor is not a widow, that her sons are far from being orphans, but she sweeps aside your objections with a wave of her hand.

Noor is on the wrong side of the fence however you look at it, according to Amina. She's had no man to share her bed since the encounter with the stranger, her sons are allowed to run free, they might as well be orphans. And as for Moha, you can't consider him a proper husband. He doesn't piss outside her house anymore, doesn't eat from her pot, doesn't relieve his needs in her crack. Noor is worse off than a widow, she has no memories of life as a married woman to speak of. Moha was always out all day, he only came home to top up on raki, or to beat his sons or accuse his wife of having put an evil spell on him. He blamed her for his gambling losses, said his luck changed as soon as he married her.

As if in response to your unspoken doubts, Amina searches through her pocket and pulls out an official document, a faded, crumpled certificate of widowhood for you to use as evidence that Noor is a widow, her three sons orphans.

Amina stole it from the town hall, from the records of another woman, a widow who's been dead for twenty years. No one will bother to check. The photo doesn't matter. Veiled women all look the same anyway.

'And the confirmation of death, written here in black and white?'

'Just cross it out,' declares Amina, who seems to have an answer for everything.

'And what if Moha finds out? I'll end up in prison alongside Noor.'

'Better that than being stoned,' she says reassuringly.

You don't know whether to admire her or be disgusted.

Powerless in the face of laws made by men, women turn to cunning, bluff, subterfuge, anything they can think of. They'll go to any lengths to manipulate the situation to their advantage. Amina doesn't like your worried look and tries to lighten your mood. She says no one will be any the wiser, Moha least of all. He's too busy with the opening of his casino to go rooting around in the town hall registry. His casino is like a palace. Red curtains, red carpets, red lights. An oudh player and a woman singer from the city to give it some atmosphere. Don't listen to the gossips calling it a brothel, saying the singer is a whore and Moha a pimp. For the first time in this place, someone is making an effort to move with the times. And what does he get for thanks? Instead of kissing his hands, people spit in his face.

The bus is late and Amina seems to think she must fill the time with a flood of talk. She doesn't realise you're tired. She prattles non-stop, without even looking at you, her gaze fixed on the mountain, as if the rocks are dictating the words to her. The mountain seems more like an immense wall severing Khouf from the rest of the world. The bus appears round the bend and Amina gives you a kiss, stuffing a thyme-flavoured biscuit in your pocket. Thyme sharpens the wits, she tells you. 'You'll need it', she shouts, waving a handkerchief, as if you were leaving for America.

Through the window of the bus the desert that unfolds before you has left its mark on everything it touches: palm trees arching towards the ground, façades of the rare shacks that dot the road, faces of people selling bottles of Coca-Cola, cups of warm water, a handful of nuts, all are the colour of sand. Holes in the ground have become lakes, transformed by the last rains. A young girl, her bracelets jangling on her skinny wrists, counts them off, counts again and tells you there are seven lakes, seven, like the days of the week. The bangles are part of her dowry, her *moukaddam*. The man she is to marry is meeting her at the end of the line. She hasn't met him yet. The old man sitting next to the driver is his father.

'And what if you don't like him?'

'Impossible.'

Her laugh echoes the jingling of her bangles.

'Do you give him back the bracelets if he doesn't marry you?'

'His father would have to marry me and I'd keep the bracelets. No one wants a woman who goes back to her parents' home a virgin.'

And the toad will spit its venom in her belly. She'll be barren.

The driver has been staring at you in the mirror. When the bus stops, he hands you a headscarf.

'You'll need it,' he whispers, 'for your meeting with the mullah.'

You don't need to ask him how he knew. Everyone in Khouf is talking about it. The driver gives you no encouragement, but he doesn't try to deter you either. He doesn't approve of stoning, but he has no opinions, on anything. He says he doesn't want to influence you, but he warns you to be careful and observe the basic courtesies: greet the mullah with a simple nod of the head, don't try to give him your hand, avoid looking directly at him, don't ever contradict him. You thank him, get off the bus, and think no more about him.

No need to go looking for the Home for Widows and Orphans, the bus stops right in front it. No need to knock on the door, it's wide open for the constant stream of women and children going in and out. Three women greet you, sisters. They listen to your plan, terrified.

'It's impossible,' they say with one voice. 'The mullah's guards will throw you out, they'll beat you up if you resist. The Minister of Virtue doesn't see women, only his wives. And even if he has ever accepted a woman's request to see him, a man would have been with her. But you, you're alone, with no husband, no father, no brother. Alone like a palm tree in the middle of the desert.'

'She could ask Abdul,' the eldest of the three suggests.

'A *mut'ah* marriage,' the youngest adds, 'for the duration of the visit, paid for in cash. Once it's over, both parties go back home.'

'Abdul?' you ask wearily. 'Who's Abdul?'

'The bus driver who brought you to Khouf. He always helps women in trouble, he marries them for a day, a week, depending on what they want and how much they pay.'

You hesitate. You promise to think about it and give them your answer tomorrow. The journey was exhausting; you need to find a hotel for some rest. Any hotel will do. Arms are placed around your shoulders. The women speak to you as if you were ill. You realise they are telling you that women are not allowed into hotels alone. You might find yourself having to spend the night in the street, with the dogs that descend on the city as soon as darkness falls. They roam the streets freely, driven by hunger, sinking their teeth into anything in their path, even trees and lampposts.

'Make up your mind, before Abdul leaves to go back to Khouf.'

'Alright,' you say, your voice weak with exhaustion. 'A temporary marriage. By *mut'ah*.'

Your begrudging acceptance of their plan is a source of great delight. The women surround you, touch you, kiss you on both cheeks. Children romp about, an old woman they call the cook shouts loudly, asking if three jugs of hibiscus tea, *karkade*, will be enough. Should she add a fourth?

A flurry of preparations begins. Chairs are pushed against the walls, lined up in serried ranks, just as in a house prepared to receive mourners after a death. The raised stool in the centre is your seat. You don't have to do anything. You are the bride, even though your marriage will only last an afternoon.

The youngest child hangs out of the window and calls out to a boy playing in the courtyard. She tells him to go and get Abdul and the sheikh and bring them here as quickly as he can. 'It's for a wedding,' she tells him. 'An urgent marriage.' High-pitched calls ring out all over the house as women, swathed in veils, give vent to their joy, their tongues flapping at dizzying speed in wild ululation.

Yalalalalalalala to the skies.

You venture one last question.

'What if Abdul says no?'

A wave of answers greets your question.

It's never happened. He always helps out women in need. It's no skin off his nose, he has four wives already. A fifth wife is forbidden by the Qur'an, it won't count. *Mut'ah* is only a mock marriage.

You feel as if you are at the theatre, preparing to go on stage. You have the main part. They paint your face with powder, plastering it on like shaving cream, marking your cheeks with two red circles. Rose water is sprinkled on you, mysterious shapes drawn on the palms of your hands, a spot of henna on your forehead and chin. And then your bridegroom strolls in, very much at ease, a man who marries and remarries according to supply and demand.

Abdul's only concern is that it should all be wrapped up in two hours. After that, once his bus is filled with passengers, he can do nothing to help.

You keep telling yourself you are in a play, you are the heroine, the three people presiding over the ceremony are actors on the stage, the choir. They take it in turns to speak, according to the script. They offer you neither encouragement nor discouragement; they are helping you to do what you can, to make sure you have no regrets later. The mullah and the minister, will they agree to see you? Only Allah knows. Will they beat you? Break your leg? Blind you in one eye? We cannot say what will happen. The guards

64

are heavy-handed, arms like threshers, teeth as sharp as a tiger's. The mullah is a holy man, don't forget, a man with four wives, who never shakes a woman's hand. He married in obedience to the teachings of the Qur'an, not for the pleasures of the flesh, he gives his four wives equal treatment, doesn't have a favourite. Their shoes are the same style, their veils of equal thickness so they'll see the world in the same light. They're all named Aïsha after the last of the Prophet's wives.

You interrupt their litany and tell them what you are worried about. How can you be sure Noor won't be executed before the mullah gives his judgment on her case? Their answer is the same as always. They raise their arms to heaven, no one can foresee the future. You must be prepared for the best and the worst alike.

Turning it all over in your mind, you begin to think they might be right. And then, the eldest tells you that the mullah and the minister have been known to disagree. The mullah sometimes refutes the minister's decisions; the minister does not always validate the mullah's pronouncements. If the rope is pulled in two different directions, the decision will be put off to a later date.

'And then what?' you ask in a whisper.

'Nothing.'

The Home for Widows and Orphans can do no more. What can we do? they say. We are women, men will just say it's prattle, tell us to hold our tongues, accuse us of associating with feminists from abroad, instruments of

Satan, of spreading talk of the country's problems beyond the borders. "Bells on the rear end of a donkey", the minister calls us.

They talk, one after another, oblivious to the passing of time, not seeing Abdul checking his watch, unaware of the imam arriving and demanding to be paid in advance.

A scuffle breaks out in the courtyard. Children, big and small, burst into the hall and hang on to Abdul's coat tails, his sons and daughters wanting to come to the ceremony. They'll have to be given a coin each to stop them opposing their father's marriage. Abdul himself asks nothing of you, he's doing you a favour, nothing more, but he is counting on your generosity to brighten up the children's day. No sweets though, they rot the teeth, just money. They'll give it to their mothers who will decide how it is to be spent.

Someone hands you a printed document. You don't understand much of it and just as you are about to sign, the sheikh taps the back of your hand and stops you. You must pray first. You repeat the words that come out of his mouth, write your name out in full next to Abdul's finger print, while the women in charge help themselves to the contents of your purse. 'Just to cover the cost of the document and the ink,' they explain.

And there you are, walking three paces behind him, in the customary manner, on your way to see the Minister for the Repression of Vice. An obedient wife following behind her master.

II.

You lower your voice, stare at the ground at your feet. You must not even glance at the person seated in front of you, enthroned on a red velvet Louis xv style armchair, his eyes invisible behind opaque dark glasses.

You tell him how Noor was raped, of the child she is carrying, of the lapidation delayed for the first time by the *khamsin*, and a second time by the dryness of the earth, a stoning that will make orphans of four children.

'Three,' he corrects you. 'The fourth will not yet be born.'

'One word from you,' you interject plaintively. 'And a woman who has been unjustly condemned will be able to live her life into old age.'

'What makes you think she wants to live to old age?'

You try another approach. You talk to him of her house built of mud bricks. It'll fall into ruin when she is no longer there to shore up the walls.

'You know how fragile packed earth buildings are. Her waster of a husband won't do anything to look after the house when she's gone. He'll be too busy with his new wife and his gambling.'

He cuts you off, drily: 'One crumbling building more or less. What difference does it make?'

Ruins are the inspiration for the most beautiful of Arabic poems. He starts to recite, half singing:

'Let us stop here and weep for the beloved and her house',

'Shaped by the winds, from north and from south' you continue in the same sing-song voice. You are expecting an admiring look, but he grimaces in response, curling his lips beneath the thick moustache.

He criticises your Arabic, reproaches you for reciting the words of the poet Imru' al-Qays with a French accent. You are like the quail, he says, the quail that tried to walk like a swan. Neither swan nor quail, it forgot how to walk at all.

His advice to you is to forget your western side, to be true to your Arabic self, to stop putting shameful demands into the mouths of these women.

'Our women have much to say, but they do not think. They exist and that is enough, they are happy with that. They are needed for procreation.'

In other words, they have their uses, just as saucepans, ladles and bowls do.

He dismisses you with a sweep of the hand. Continuing the exchange is out of the question. Don't make him angry, Abdul whispers to you as he drags you outside. When the door is closed behind you, you give way to despair, but

Abdul buoys you up, reassures you that all is not lost. The mullah responsible for the protection of virtue is known to be capable of great generosity. A good man. Who knows, he might rescind the sentence handed down to Noor? His judgment will challenge the findings of the Minister for the Suppression of Vice, who everyone knows has never even pissed on an injured finger.

You don't know whether to laugh or cry. After three hours of marriage and the best part of a day in Abdul's company, you've realised that he talks all the time in proverbs he doesn't bother to explain.

12.

'If it's about the stoned woman who changed the way her tombstone faces again, don't waste your time. The case is closed.'

The mullah greets you with these opening remarks.

'The woman in question is still alive, your Holiness. Unless you intervene, she will be executed.'

'And what is the problem?' he asks, visibly exasperated.

'The woman is expecting. The child will be an orphan.'

'One orphan more or less. We each come into this world with our allotted portion. The Creator will see to the child's needs.'

His words take you back to the heart-rending spectacle of children, big and small, scavenging at the rubbish dump on the outskirts of the city.

'They always find what they need to feed and clothe themselves,' a fellow passenger had said 'What does it matter if the fruit is half rotten and the clothes worn out?'

The mullah's stern voice brings you back to the here and

now: 'You're not from our country. What are you doing here?'

'Aid work', you whisper in response.

'Your organisation does more harm than good. You are to blame for the famine. Instead of tending their crops, our peasants fill their stomachs with the rice and flour you hand out to them. Proud men, and you make beggars and idlers of them.'

Your eyes are fixed on his soft leather slippers, never on the face that is forbidden to women. You say the drought is to blame for the famine, the drought alone is responsible, not idleness. The drought has ruined the harvest, killed the livestock. The lack of rain has forced the peasants into the city, the children to the rubbish dumps.

His response is not at all what you were expecting: 'Flowers need fertile soil to grow. Children are no different.'

Proud of his turn of phrase, he follows it with a proverb of his own invention:

'The devil does not applaud when Allah walks on the rubbish heap.'

Is he saying that the children at the dump are the children of God?

He's too wrapped up in himself to offer an explanation.

A long silence follows, which you dare not interrupt. He strokes his beard for the hundredth time. His gaze is fixed on the carpet, intensely scrutinising the patterns. Is he searching for God in the weave, in the web of wool and cotton threads? Suddenly, as if struck by a flash of inspiration, he asks you a question, says you should think carefully before giving your answer.

'Which do you prefer, the road or the horse?'

What is he playing at? You don't know which to opt for. He gloats at your silence and the defeat it implies.

You shake your head three times, exhausted to the point of collapse. Scarcely able to hold back your tears, you confess that you don't know.

'To put it more clearly,' he declares, in the thundering tones of a preacher. 'Is it this woman's life you wish to save, or her soul?'

You feel yourself staggering, collapsing on the carpet. Your lips brush the slipper of his right foot, as if you are about to kiss it.

He stretches his hand out to you and orders you to get up. A crisp command emanating from the opening between the beard and moustache.

'Stand up.' As if you were Lazarus and he Christ.

What are you waiting for? Why don't you leave now? Two failed attempts in one day? But you are brought back to reality by his voice. As a demonstration of his infinite generosity, the mullah will put off the date of the stoning until later, until after the birth of the child, even though the child is the rotted fruit of a rotten tree and common sense would suggest the tree should be cut down at the root. 'The tree and its rotten fruit with it', he adds.

He hands you a paper adorned with his signature

surmounted by an unsheathed dagger.

'Give this to the sheikh of Khouf and tell him: "This is the will of the mullah. No stoning until after the birth of the child."

You go back outside. The street buzzes with the sound of horns, with the cries of men selling ice creams, syrups, peanuts, biscuits, sticks of incense, birds fluttering around in cages, stuffed birds. Not a single shop selling women's clothing. Burqas are made in backstreet workshops. Even a dress by itself, empty of contents, could be suggestive of naked flesh. Woman must remain hidden from sight, confined to the darkness of the bedchamber, fit only to be impregnated and perpetuate mankind.

13.

Snow begins to fall as the bus pulls out, fine light snow-flakes that melt as they touch the ground, floating down so slowly they seem to be suspended in the air. The landscape disappears, crushed beneath a great weight. Lulled by the rocking motion of the bus, you think of Noor waiting for your return, wondering whether you will bring reprieve or death for her.

All talk on the bus is of the wave of cold air sweeping down from Siberia, replacing the drought that came up from the Sahel. Sleepy voices ask the bus to stop and with every request, Abdul pulls off to the side of the road and climbs on the roof to throw a bag down to its owner. As the figures retreat into the blinding whiteness, you wonder where they are going. The bus trundles on, the snow falling more thickly as you advance into the night, the light dusting that fell on the suburbs now a thick blanket obliterating all the villages along the route. You feel as if you have been travelling forever, that Khouf is at the end of the world. An icy wind whips around your skirt every time the door is opened. You shiver. Abdul gazes at you protectively, wraps his blanket around you.

'My wedding gift', he whispers in your ear.

The bus arrives in the village square and the few remaining passengers scatter in different directions, leaving you alone with Abdul. You refuse his offer to go with you to the Centre but keep the blanket, your protection from the cold. Abdul will stretch out on the back seat, gazing up at the stars, dreaming of his wives: not of you, the wife by *mu'tah*, but the four legitimate wives who will greet him with open arms tomorrow when he arrives back in the city.

You walk briskly, striding through the silence punctuated by the barking of dogs. The crunch of your feet sinking into the soft snow sounds to you like the croaking of toads on a hot night. You walk on blindly, guided by the outline of the Barbary fig half buried in the white mass.

The good news you bring for Noor cannot wait until tomorrow. You arrive in front of her house, but something is wrong. You wonder if you have made a mistake. The building with the gaping hole at the front bears no resemblance to your friend's house. In the darkness, a shadow appears, urging you to go inside before the cold turns you to stone.

'Not until you've guessed what I've got in my hand', you say.

'How am I supposed to guess?'

'Just try.'

'You've won the lottery? You've inherited some money? You've found a husband?'

With each question from Noor you shake your head. She grows increasingly annoyed, not understanding how a mere piece of paper can put you into such a state.

Aware of the importance of what you are about to reveal, you speak slowly, enunciating each syllable.

You tell her that no one will touch a hair on her head until after the birth of the baby.

'And then what?' she asks bitterly, full of pride and disdain.

Her question cuts right through you, her eyes probing yours through the darkness.

Hands on hips in a gesture of defiance, she asks you who will nurse the baby, keep him warm, sing him to sleep with lullabies. What's the point of coming into the world on the day his mother's head is split open by hundreds of rocks?

'I'll try again with the mullah, now that I know the way', you say, dismayed or perhaps shamed by her question.

She thinks before answering, her finger glued to her temple. Smiling suggestively, she asks if you and the imam are... and she crosses her fingers.

A blush spreads over your face but she pays no attention. She probably cannot see it in the darkness. Suddenly she is full of her plans: there's nothing to stop her planting vegetables now that she has life to look forward to.

'And why not some flowers?' she adds. 'This garden is as sad as the desert.'

Is Noor laughing at you, or at herself?

For the first time she makes the familiar pregnant woman's gesture as she places her brown hand on her belly. Normally so silent, Noor is suddenly garrulous. She wants to see her sons to tell them of the birth of their little brother, she wants her arms to be long enough to embrace them all at the same time, she wants to feed them, watch them devouring saffron rice, turmeric lamb stew, mountains of cakes. Even last year's chicken, plucked and eaten more than a year ago, is included in her plans: she says she will cook it on a slow fire until the flesh falls away from the bones.

The lamb, the turmeric, the chicken, all nothing but the cravings of a pregnant woman. Exhausted from talking she lapses into silence. You seize the chance to ask her what has happened to her front door.

'Moha asked me for it. He lost his in a card game. If you think about it though, the door belongs to him. He was the one who paid the carpenter'. She paces up and down the room. 'Just so long as he leaves me the window.'

Holding her head up defiantly, she declares she prefers the house without the door anyway. All it did was block her view of the mountain and stop her seeing the lights of the village coming on one by one as darkness fell.

You know the reality is not so simple. It is true that Moha gambled away his own door, but he took Noor's front door to punish her. A punishment for the journey you were making to plead for her life. A wife, even one that has been disowned, has no business complaining of her fate to an outsider. A good wife does not contest a fatwa from the sheikh. A good Muslim woman, worthy of the name, refuses any attempt to intervene on her behalf against the laws of her people.

You are too exhausted to take exception to her ramblings. Your head nods forward on to your chest, your legs are too weak to carry you back to the Centre. She tells you to stay, offers you her own bedding, wishes you sweet dreams. Your eyes close as she tries to block up the gaping hole with a piece of metal sheeting she found thrown against her Barbary fig by the wind. She busies herself lighting the fire, gathering up the coals with her nimble fingers and placing them between the twigs. All she needs to do is blow on it. Her narrow chest seems to contain all the winds of the desert. Her youthful frame has already given birth to three children and is carrying a fourth; a *weled*, as she had announced after her pilgrimage to Sitt Zeinab's well. A boy, for a girl counts for nothing. And yet it's the girls that command a high price in marriage: a herd of goats, an item of furniture for the parents, sometimes even hard cash.

It's the women you've seen digging the cracked soil in search of roots to put in the stew, the women who knead mud and straw to patch up the walls. And all the while, the men sit talking under a tree, throwing out words of advice, sometimes aiming a stone at the head of those who turn a deaf ear.

Sleep arrives quickly as you burrow under the blanket with its whiff of camel. You dream you are being carried across the desert in a caravan. You have been expelled from Khouf for intervening in the lives of the locals, and you have no other way to get back to France. As you jolt along on the palanquin, your body flinches with every lurch of the elderly beast you've been assigned. Perhaps they are hoping she will ditch you into a ravine and you'll never be heard of again. You cry out in your sleep, waking Noor who is huddled in a corner. She hurries to your side, soothes your forehead with her hand, her lips forming threats in choice language to the devil, the father of all nightmares. As you wake from your sleep, she gives you a sip of orange blossom water to calm you, a cup of coffee to bring you back to your senses. You don't protest. You'll need it to face the sheikh. Anxious, you worry. He must be persuaded to follow the mullah's orders. So long as he has not seen the holy man's signature with his own eyes, Noor's life will still be in danger.

She returns to the events of the day before, asks you to tell her again what happened, not to omit the smallest detail.

'What did the mullah say, foreign woman?'

'He said the final decision to exonerate you is in the hands of Allah, who weaves and unweaves all things.'

Her face lights up:

'He means the gates of paradise will be open to me?'

Her tears flow for the first time since you have known her. They must be tears of joy, she cannot cry when she is sad. Dizzy with happiness, she drinks all the coffee in her pot. She can't keep still and spins around like a top, casting about with her eyes to find something, anything to give you to show her gratitude. Her hand lights on a piece of cloth knotted at either end. She pulls out a charm attached to a thick cord, places it around your neck. To protect you from the evil eye, from hostile tongues, from snakes even.

'Go in peace. Now you are protected, you have nothing more to fear,' she exclaims ardently.

She will not eat or sleep until you return. As long as there is light in the sky, she will keep watch for your silhouette at her window. She will prepare you a feast of cactus leaves cooked in oil with onions, a feast fit for a king. Envious eyes will be eaten up with jealousy.

14.

Amina has not slept a wink all night. She waited up for you until the muezzin's first call to prayer, a thousand black thoughts running through her mind. You missed the bus, you slept in the street with the dogs and beggars, you are languishing in a prison cell, arrested for getting mixed up in matters that don't concern you. Or worst of all: you've been murdered and there is no one to say who you are or which country you are from.

Yes, murdered. With the city streets full of beggars, murderers, whores, why not?

Her worst fears allayed, she asks you to tell her everything.

Did you see the Minister for the Suppression of Vice at close quarters, is it true that he has a glass eye? Did the mullah responsible for upholding virtue agree to see you? What did he say about Noor?

'She's been given a stay of execution, until after the birth, possibly for ever', you reply. 'But I have to persuade the sheikh. You must come with me to the mosque.'

A shiver runs down her spine.

'You'll have to go alone. He mustn't know I'm working for the French, with the aid workers.'

You remind her that he regularly syphons off twenty percent of the supplies meant for the destitute of Khouf.

'Do you know what he does with it?'

Of course she knows. Counting them off on her fingers, she rattles off the names of the sheikh's four wives and their sixteen children.

'Eight boys, seven girls and one half and half, neither fish nor fowl.'

She doesn't like your wary look. You can go alone, she concedes, men of Allah are above suspicion, you can look after yourself. She'll meet you at Noor's house. Without her door, Noor's in danger of being devoured by wild animals, murdered by thieves.

'Robbers? In the village?' you say, surprised.

'Why not? A thief is a thief wherever you are. They'll steal the walls if they can't find anything else to take.'

The people of Khouf may be poor in food, you muse, but they are certainly rich in arguments.

You think of the people at the Centre in the mornings from the moment the doors open, hands outstretched towards the sacks of food, held upwards to God, who seems to have forgotten them. Or are they pleading with the clouds that refuse to rain? They know the snow will soon vanish, sucked up by the thirsty soil and by the sun that nothing can assuage.

An old man claimed he had dug all the way down to hell in search of a stream that had always been there. All he found was water so muddy even the animals refused it. 'Devil's spit', his wife had added. 'Better to die of thirst than drink that stuff.'

Jalila, the eternal malcontent, had given back your bag of lentils half empty telling you she'd found a stone in the lentils. She almost broke her tooth on it. She opened her mouth wide to show you and pointed to three wobbly stumps, two above, one below.

Their complaints wound on, coiling like a rope around your neck. You went outside to breathe. Above your head, hundreds of gulls were flying low in the sky. Seagulls, so far from the sea.

'They're going to tear the clouds with their beaks,' a little boy shouted. 'It's going to rain'. But no one was listening. No one looked up at the sky.

15.

Amina tries to warn you against Jalila. Lying comes as easily to her as begging, she says. You shouldn't believe a word Jalila says about Mecca, she's never been anywhere near it. All she did was dream she saw the Kaaba in the desert, coming towards her like a camel trying to make its way back to its caravan. Jalila thinks she's a *hajja*, but the only pilgrimage she's made to Mecca is in her dreams. She's never set foot outside of Khouf.

Noor is no gossip, but she agrees with Amina. Jalila claims that long ago, before time began, Khouf was under the sea, that the desert was once an ocean, the dunes, islands. But it's all lies. The coating of age-old soot on her cooking pot is proof enough for Noor that Khouf existed before the earth and the sky.

Hamidou, the warehouse foreman, doesn't think much of Jalila either. He says she looks at the sacks of food with her evil eye and pierces holes in them, like rats with their teeth. You let them rattle on. You will never turn Jalila away, for the simple reason that she always smells of the cats that seek refuge behind her ample back at night when the dogs are on the hunt for them.

Jalila comes every morning at the same time, Hamidou tells you, with her dustpan and brush. She goes around sweeping and picking up whatever she can, flour, sugar, anything that's leaked from the bags, and then sells it to the people of the village, at cut-price rates, to people she claims are worse off than she is, poorer than her, Jalila, the poorest of us all.

Sugar and flour, tasted on the thumb to test for rat poison. Jalila, the rubbish bin nutritionist, the unwitting ecologist, sifting out the rotting fruits and vegetables from people's waste in the days when food in Khouf was plentiful. Never meat, she was disgusted at the idea. 'Like eating your neighbour.' She asked you yesterday, looking you straight in the eye, if you'd ever eaten donkey meat. She changed the subject when she saw how appalled you looked, and told you her favourite dish was stale bread soaked in sugar water. She places it on her head first, just as the prophet Ali instructs, then on her Qur'an until it is purified, then softens it with a touch of orange blossom. A feast fit for a king, she declared, licking her lips.

'You have a copy of the Qur'an?' you asked, knowing that Jalila can't read.

'And why wouldn't I have one?'

She pulled three musty, tattered pages from her pocket, their edges jagged, rescued from dustbins. Which verses are they, which suras? Jalila doesn't know. She just knows they are from the Book. She pressed them to her bony chest, then put them on her head, holding her breath to stop them falling on the ground. To keep them from Satan, lord of everything here below. On high, everything belongs to the *malaïkas*, the angels who have nothing to do but fly around day and night.

Exasperated, trying not to laugh, you gazed at her impassively.

She closed her eyes to escape your gaze, or perhaps to avoid the eyes of Satan. Her wrinkled lips muttered a prayer, a single phrase filled with exhortations to the devil to stay away from her house.

Jalila's home is the street, all of it. When sleep overcomes her, she lies down on the spot, her eyes rolling around in their sockets like crazed marbles. She finds a wall to slump against, imagines it multiplied by four, adds a roof to the four walls. Having a house of her own doesn't interest her: Khouf will be drowned soon anyway beneath millions of cubic metres of water once the construction of the dam is complete. She is the only one who realises, the only one to speak of it. Who else in the village has heard the noise from the works on the other side of the mountain? The sounds of rock being dynamited are hidden from all but her old ears. The dam is being constructed by invisible men from another planet, Jalila says categorically. She knows because she sleeps outside, she's the only one who can see them.

You wonder how she comes up with all of this. But it's no different from what Noor thinks: she'd probably claim the man who made love to her the night of the *khamsin* came from the same planet.

She'd said as much yesterday, barely suppressing a shiver of fear, of desire.

16.

The snow that fell the night you came back from the capital has melted everywhere except for Noor's garden. Using a wooden spoon, she clears the snow and digs evenly spaced holes, filling them with red, black and yellow seeds, which she spits on before covering them with earth. She works with her eyes closed to avoid giving her seeds the evil eye, spitting on the devil to ensure her plants grow straight and strong. When the seeds are all gone, she gives a sigh of satisfaction, stands up straight holding her back with both hands, and turns her gaze towards the front of her house: two meters by four of dried mud, crumbling away a little more each winter, walls scarred by wrinkles and scratches. Like her face. Houses in town, she's heard, show no signs of age, nor do the women. The salt-laden sea air protects them, preserves them in brine. They have a cure for everything in the city, even poverty.

You think of the children you saw scavenging in the stinking rubbish heaps, but say nothing.

Perhaps it is the whiteness of the snow that's giving you this tranquil feeling. Here on the edge of the desert with Noor and Amina, you imagine you are three women, no different from any others, without a care in the world. Amina, not on the shelf, or too old to find a husband. No death sentence hanging over Noor. And you, not abandoned by a lover, your cat still alive. Three of you, chatting calmly about this and that, your voices lingering in the air. Voices coming from mouths that aren't yours.

The mountain takes hold of the sun and Noor drags you inside. She lights the fire and as you gaze at the flames in the hearth, a gentle drowsiness comes over you. Noor and Amina prattle on, the sound of their voices lulling you into a half-sleep. Thinking you cannot hear them, they talk freely about you.

'She has the minister's ear, and the mullah's too,' Noor tells Amina, 'even though she's Christian.'

'She married Abdul and that makes her a Muslim,' Amina counters.

'That camel? How do you know she married him?'

'I heard it from him, the husband. As soon as he arrived in the village he trumpeted it from the rooftops. Even the dead must have heard him.'

'Do you think she'll move in with him?'

'Where do you think he would put her? With four wives and a dozen brats. And besides, marriage by *mut'ah* doesn't give you the right to a roof over your head.'

A silence follows, then Noor's child-like voice slipping

in and out of the crackling of the fire. She'd love to know why you have taken her case to heart, why you want to save her from death, if the aid-workers are there for a reason. Amina sweeps aside her questions with a wave of the hand. The only reason the aid-workers are there is to give out food, drink and vaccinations. She suspects the feminists of being behind your campaign. You are simply following orders from Paris. These women are powerful. They are in charge; men are under their boots. They do whatever they feel like, driving cars, trains, lorries, they organise demonstrations, smoke…

'Hashish?' Noor gasps.

'Worse than hashish. Cigarettes. They drink too.'

'What, raki?'

'Whatever is in their glass, even if it's forbidden by the Qur'an. Wine.'

'Not the foreign woman,' declares Noor, full of admiration. 'I've never seen her drinking or smoking. You'd think she was a *hajja* with several pilgrimages to Mecca to her name.'

'So many good qualities, but no husband in sight,' Amina bemoans.

'No husband, but she does have a fiancé.'

'You call him a fiancé but he was just a lover who left her to go back to his wife.'

'And she rejected him,' Noor continues.

'Just as well for him,' they say in one voice.

'So a woman can reject a man where she comes from?'

Noor enquires.

'Where she comes from, and just about everywhere else except Khouf. Women can have any job they want, from whore to president of the Republic.'

'And there are brothels for women too?'

Noor is insatiable in her thirst to know, Amina happy to invent answers.

'On every street corner. The more you pay, the younger and more attractive the man you get, especially if he's blond. Your Moha, scrawny creature that he is, he'd have to satisfy himself with a goat. No woman would want him. Not like Abdul. He'd be so much in demand, he wouldn't be able to keep up.'

'He's no handyman either, my Moha,' Noor complains sorrowfully. 'He can't even hammer a nail into the wall.'

'He managed to plant three brats in your belly,' Amina reminds her. 'And what makes you so sure the French woman's man was any good with a hammer and nails?'

'How do you expect me to know? All I know about him is that he knows how to paint. If he wasn't so far away, he'd have repainted these walls. All that grime that's been accumulating as long as this house has been standing.'

'You call this a house,' Amina retorts. 'But it's nothing but a dilapidated hut. And as for the foreign woman's fiancé, it's pictures he paints, pictures to hang on walls: blue sky, trees, birds...'

'No flowers?' Noor asks. 'I love flowers. The world wouldn't be the same without flowers.'

'Not that I know of, she'd have said.'

'My Moha doesn't know the first thing about drawing flowers.'

'Nor does Abdul, nor any man in Khouf,' Amina reassures her. 'When Allah got to the end of his work he must have run out of clay to make top-quality men. He cobbled something together and got by with what he could lay his hands on, the same mud for the men as for the houses. Rough to touch, not like the Frenchies, all nice and smooth.'

'All that washing makes them even smoother. They wash morning and evening, even when there's a drought or when the *khamsin* is up, even when the wells have run dry.'

'Do they even have wells?'

'They have all Allah's creations except for camels and grasshoppers. Abdul should know all about it now that he's married the French woman.'

'Do you think he's had her yet?'

'No time for that, he's out all day and half the night.'

'It's within his rights though. He could have insisted. A hundred strokes of the cane for the woman who refuses her husband. Maybe he got put off, can't be easy to undress these woman with their tight trousers, you could end up peeling off their skin.'

'Shhh, don't talk so loud,' says Noor. 'I think she can hear us.'

'She's asleep. You can see it in her feet, they've turned white. There's a grain of death in sleep.'

'And a lot of sleep in death,' Noor continues as if inspired.

You try hard not to laugh. Lulled by their voices you let their talk wash over you, accepting it all unquestioningly. Barely a month ago, you would have considered such ideas primitive. But here, so far from your country, from your friends and the man you loved, you live in harmony with these women, gradually going along with their superstitions. As you become closer to them, the west recedes. All that is left of your old life is a small garden that has probably died for lack of water, the panicked mewling of a cat as evening falls, and a bay window in the grey drizzle. People vanish into the mouth of the metro, lop-sided figures with one shoulder dipped below the other from carrying bags, food, children. The west, carrying the weight of the world on its shoulders.

17.

The weather has suddenly turned warmer. All that remains of the snow are a few patches of frost forgotten by the sun. Amina walks along behind you, grumbling incessantly. Noor's cooking is sitting heavily in her stomach. All those lentils and chick peas. Not the grilled chicken she'd been dreaming of, the stuffed lamb or at the very least, vegetables, slow-cooked courgettes and aubergines. She feels more and more bloated, blown up like a watermelon, she'll be rolling along the ground soon instead of walking.

'Don't blame Noor', you tell her reminding her that nothing grows in Khouf except cactus and thistles, food for donkeys.

'For donkeys and the people who live here,' she says bitterly.

She stops abruptly, one hand on your arm, pointing to a pile of stones. Rooted to the spot on a patch of frost, she stares at the stones, aghast.

'Did you give the mullah's letter to the sheikh?'

You confess that he refused to see you, that he sent you back to the qadi.

'And what did he say, the qadi?'

'That stoning Noor is no one's business but her husband's. He more or less threw me out. All he was interested in was the cock fight he was judging.'

'Cowards, all of them,' she says, spitting on the ground to underline her disgust.

All thoughts of stuffed lamb and chicken are instantly forgotten, no more talk of courgettes and aubergines. She rolls up her sleeves and asks you to help her clear away the stones.

Like two mechanical dolls, you bend down; moving together as one, you take hold of the rocks and hurl them towards the surrounding fields. You don't stop until all the stones are gone. Bathed in sweat, you shiver, from the cold but mostly from the fear of being caught. Now that the heap of stones lies scattered about the fields, Noor will be spared from stoning.

You arrive at Noor's house in high spirits, both demanding to be fed. Hungrily, you devour the lentil soup and chick pea salad, Amina lapping up the last drops in the bowl. As you chew, Noor chatters to you about her garden, her baby, talking of the child, courgettes and aubergines in the same breath. The glow of the fire illuminates your faces, Noor's bony features, Amina's face as round as the gibbous moon, yours palid and mask-like in comparison. You hear a noise from the direction of the village, growing louder and louder as it approaches. You look outside and see a crowd, armed with torches lining up beyond the hedge. Flames, mouths clamouring. Demanding reparation. Ordering Noor to put the heap of stones back as it was or they will burn her alive. You and Amina are ready to confront the crowd, but Noor sends you back inside. She stands unflinching before the howling mob, parrying the insults with silence. A statue, clothed in dignity, dressed in rags, staring over their heads at the road beyond.

Is she hoping to discern the outline of the man who made her pregnant? The commotion suddenly dies down, silenced by her composure. Shouts and calls for her death shatter as they fall to the ground. People leave, carrying their torches. A crowd of forty, maybe fifty. Children. The cowardly people of Khouf have sent their children.

A cloud of fireflies darts from the Barbary fig, alarmed by the sound of footsteps. They hurl themselves at the lamp. Noor adjusts the wick, reproaching you for dismantling the heap of stones. To lay a hand on such a burial mound is tantamount to demolishing a tomb, she says, her voice as faint as the fire in the hearth struggling to ignite.

18.

Noor sniffs the tiny green shoots in her garden. She knows them all by their smell: the acidic tang of tomato, sweet-smelling courgette, spicy basil, and aubergine with its whiff of cigarette smoke. The days of waiting for death are long gone, the tawdry scene clumsily enacted by children at their parents' behest is forgotten. Her plants keep pace with the child growing in her womb. To celebrate the appearance of the green shoots she spring-cleans the house, treats herself to a bath. The sheikh and the qadi have lost interest in her. They have their hands full since a young girl was raped on her way to draw water from the well.

'The night it snowed,' Noor informs you.

The girl comes to the Centre, flanked by her parents, the whole village following in their wake. Boys snigger, girls giggle, their hands over their mouths: it's not just rape, she is four months pregnant. But Dr. Paul is adamant: it didn't snow until two weeks ago.

The girl is unable to describe her assailant; her father

speaks on her behalf. The man who raped her looked like a European, he drove a jeep. The wife says it was the devil. The devil made her daughter pregnant. People are inclined to believe the mother, no one believes the father. He made it all up, the man with the jeep hasn't set foot in the village for months. The project he was working on ran out of funds, the works have closed down. The sacks of supplies allotted to him are still sitting in the warehouse. The spokesman for the villagers says he was a respectable man, polite and well-mannered.

You think of the man who made love to Noor, while the sand swirled around them, the *khamsin* whipping up showers of needles to lacerate their flesh, their bodies fused together in passion, in mutual desire.

Questioning the girl without her parents present leads nowhere. She simply stares back, silent and terrified.

That evening, when they have all left, Dr. Paul looks pained, but his assistant thinks it was a great joke. Gonzagues has a low opinion of the villagers, he has no desire to be of use to any of them. The earth is not so hard now that it's snowed, the people will be able to till the soil, sew their seeds, harvest their crops. It's time for the westerners to pack their bags and leave, move on.

Surprisingly, the doctor agrees. He is weary of dragging himself from one country to another, tired of battling against hunger, drought, Third World diseases. He's ready to go back to his house that looks out on to the sea, to his wife, his children and grandchildren.

A wave of cold grips your chest. With the aid-workers gone, you'd have no choice but to leave Noor to her fate: at the mercy of the sheikh and the people of Khouf. What if they were to revive the fatwa hanging over her? The decision to move out renders you speechless. You want to oppose it but your words stick in your throat. You can only shake your head. No one asks your opinion, but still you go on shaking your head.

19.

Plunged into disarray by your colleagues' decision to leave Khouf, you wander aimlessly through the village, following the single line of buildings from the town hall at the top to the cemetery at the bottom. You pass the last of the houses and strike out across the fields, away from the hostile stares of children and dogs. There are no adults to be seen. They're all inside their houses where they can turn a deaf ear to their squabbling children. Yesterday a little boy fell over in front of you. You picked him up, wiped the blood from his knee with your handkerchief and produced a sweet from your pocket. He stopped crying and a crowd formed around you. Thirty or more little hands clutched at your skirt. You promised to come back, but none of them really believed you. They followed you to the very edge of the village, calling out to you, their voices filled with the same rancour you heard the night they charged up to Noor's house bearing their torches and threatening to burn down the house and the woman inside.

You burst into Dr. Paul's office, perhaps to escape the children, and find him organising his files in preparation for the impending closure of the Centre. Or perhaps it is from a desire to offer them a better life that you feel compelled to ask him to leave the files for you. You'll need them, you say.

He blinks. 'I'm staying in Khouf,' you announce by way of explanation.

'To do what?'

'I'm going to open a school.'

'A school? In the desert? What do you intend to use for a building?'

'The warehouse will do.'

'A school without seats, desks, pens or pencils? You'll never find a teacher to come and work in this god-forsaken place.'

'I'll teach them. Amina will help me. The children will sit on the ground, on mats. You'll send us books, paper, pencils. Lots of pencils.'

'And who will pay you?'

You scratch your head, searching for an answer, only to hear Amina announce as she appears:

'The children's parents will pay, in fruit and vegetables. Now that it's rained.'

You fall into each other's arms once again, weeping with the emotion of it all, while the doctor peers at you short-sightedly. He is stunned, unable to make any sense of your decision. He knows nothing of your fear of going back home to an empty house, of abandoning Noor to her fate.

You were wrong to think you hated Khouf. Now that you have decided to stay, you feel regenerated. Suddenly your work weighs less heavily on you. No demands are too much. The most improbable of confidences seem entirely reasonable to you. Your role is to listen, to find solutions to problems.

The muezzin complains that his son will be incapable of succeeding him. The boy had mumps, received no treatment, his testicles are damaged. His voice hasn't broken. He knows you will have a solution. You hand him some of Dr. Paul's cough syrup and he thanks you profusely. Tomorrow he will dedicate his first prayer to you.

An old man comes to you with a request that throws you into confusion: his turban was torn off by the wind, can you bring it back? You promise to go and look for it one evening. A mother of three children with jaundice complains that the mullah's charm is not working. The mullah is a holy man. He wrote the paper in his own hand, dipped it in water from the well before giving it to the three children to swallow. It didn't work, the children are still the colour of sand, of the *khamsin*, as yellow as the coats of the dogs in Khouf. Old Jalila dismisses the pills you offer, advocates an onion soup poultice around the waist.

You never object, never show disapproval. You are prepared to accept all their beliefs, to act as both teacher and doctor. Anything to stay close to Noor.

20.

They've left, taking their meagre baggage with them, their stethoscopes, blood-pressure cuffs, syringes all packed away. Ever since armed gangs plundered the food supplies on the road between Khouf and the capital, there's been no reason for them to stay. Finding themselves no better off than the people they were supposedly helping, they made the decision to leave. Dr. Paul went to Brittany, Gonzagues to Paris, and the rest of the team are scattered among other NGOs. The old doctor kept on trying to dissuade you right up until the last moment. How can you hope to stand up to the sheikh and the qadi? The sheikh disapproves of your stubborn insistence on saving Noor from death and the qadi accuses you of turning people away from the Sharia. Both of them refused to see you when you came with the letter from the mullah: 'Let her wait outside,' they commanded, their voices resonating with the anger of the ages.

Noor and Amina are the only ones who want you here in Khouf. Parents frowned on your change of role, disapproved of you becoming the teacher and taking charge of the medicines left behind. But they seem happy enough to send you their children, whether it is to spy on you or just to get them out of their hair.

You shed no tears as the vehicle carrying the old doctor and his team departed. All your crying was done the day your man left you, the day you buried your cat with your own hands in a corner of your garden. 'Khouf has no love for you,' old Jalila declared. 'Khouf has no love for your glassy blue eyes that reflect the sky.'

Khouf cannot love, you tell yourself. Marooned between desert and city, buffeted from drought to deluge, from heatwave to frost, the people of Khouf have hearts as stony as the soil they tread beneath their feet. Embittered since their mountain was silenced, no longer ringing to the sound of their pickaxes. Embittered and joyless since the caravans bearing spices, sandalwood, salt and silk criss-crossing the desert ceased to pause in their village square. Where once camel drivers rested their charges, now there are only beggars at the mercy of the winds that reshape the dunes as they please. Wayward blasts that change direction in an instant, concealing blizzards, becoming the *khamsin*.

Even wild beasts stay away from Khouf, Jalila says. The animals are so scrawny, wolves would rather starve than attack them. Foxes aren't interested in hens that are nothing but feathers. Jalila hates Khouf. She wasn't born here, she was born on the other side of the mountain. Before Khouf existed, before there were deserts, some say. She can make no sense of your stubborn desire to save Noor, who won't be the first woman to be stoned, nor the last.

Even Noor wonders why you are so determined to save her. You tell her you have met her husband and she is dumbfounded.

'You saw him in broad daylight? Just the two of you, and he didn't beat you, didn't break your leg, give you a black-eye?'

'Not at all. He even said he doesn't care whether you live or die, now that he's a rich man.'

'Moha? Rich?'

She shakes with laughter from head to foot. What a joke! The latest she's heard of Moha is that he's sold both his windows as well as her door to pay his gambling debts.

'What else did he say?' she asks, anxious to hear everything.

'Business is booming apparently. He insisted on taking me to see his so-called casino. It's just a little house like any other, perched on the edge of the desert. Not much to look at, but I've seen worse. He has a roulette wheel, an old ablution basin. Someone has rigged it up on a centrifuge for him. You touch it and it starts to go round, it stops whenever it feels like it on one of the numbers marked in chalk. The men squat round it on the dirt floor, watching the numbers without taking their eyes off the basin, their eyes going round in time with it, holding their breath as it spins. Anyone who tries to cheat by blowing on the ball is thrown out.

They stand up and shout that they're the winner, or the loser, their *sirwals* flapping around their legs like flags in the wind. The victor is carried on the others' shoulders all the way to the tavern where it's drinks all round. Raki and palm wine flow in abundance. And if they can't get their hands on alcohol, they make do with *eau de Cologne*.'

Noor asks one last question, still on the same track.

'Just how rich is he, my Moha?'

'Rich enough to order two new windows from the joiner,' you reply without a second thought.

21.

Standing in front of the blackboard rigged up by Abdul, you repeat for the third time the first three letters of the alphabet to the three pupils sitting cross-legged on the ground. The other children prefer to keep their distance, watching from the doorway or perched on the windowsill. Their spokesman, a tall, shaven-headed lad of about twelve, says they'll make up their minds when they have had a chance to think about it.

A, B, C, one letter for each child. Three little angels stare at you wide-eyed, no sound coming from their lips. You wonder if their brains are addled by the stifling air in the warehouse, for it's the children standing in the doorway who answer. Perhaps the air outside is more conducive to learning.

'Well done!' you say.

The outside group exchange glances, excitedly crossing the threshold, pushing and shoving to claim a place in the front row and get as close as they can to the blackboard, which seems to fascinate them. Feeling encouraged, you write more letters and still more, then look around for a sponge to erase them with. There are no sponges in Khouf, but a tuft of grass handed to you by the shaven-headed boy works just as well. He puffs up his chest with pride, filling out his tee-shirt emblazoned with the words Bin Laden in black and white.

'Do you know who Bin Laden is?'

They bite their lips. No one knows.

The tee-shirts they are wearing for their first day in school have come from the sheikh. Everyone in Khouf is kitted out in new clothes today.

You cast your eyes over the children's chests and see more illustrious names, some with slogans: "*Castro por la vida*", "*Che Guevara no muerto*". And seated side by side: "*I Love America*" and "*Fuck Bush*".

Castro, Guevara? Do they know these names? No, they've never heard of them, but they do know Bush. They can draw him with their eyes closed, with a tail long enough to go three times around the school. Bush al-Satan.

Then, without asking to be excused, they leave. Hunger calls and the smell of rice cooked in cumin and turmeric is as commanding as the sound of the muezzin's voice calling them to prayer. Restored to their full vitality by the sharpness of the air outside, the children push and shove each other playfully, calling out to each other by name. You hear voices call Zahi, Zad, Zein, but you cannot say which of the twenty boys are Noor's sons.

They scatter in all directions, leaving you alone with the shaven-headed boy, who seems to have decided he's your assistant ever since he helped you out with his tuft of dried grass. There's been no sign of Amina all morning. Did she send him in her place? That would explain why he's been shaking out the mat so vigorously, sweeping the floor and sprinkling it with water from the earthenware jug. He will go back home later this afternoon when he's no longer needed. His village is on the other side of the mountain, near the dam they're building, although work has been stopped for the time being. The engineer has left for France, but he's left his jeep and his work clothes. He'll be back.

So much information and you haven't asked a single question. You encourage him to keep you updated on the man with the jeep if he hears any more news.

The boy's name is Rahim. He leaves the village when the sun begins to sink towards the horizon, not on foot as you expected but on a donkey, his very own beast that he leaves tethered to the trunk of a palm tree. He straddles it in one leap and sets off in a great clacking of hooves, just like any kid in Paris on his moped, the donkey's jubilant hee-haw filling the air like the popping of a motorbike's exhaust.

As darkness falls, earlier than usual, you wonder what has happened to Amina. She's unmarried, and she's not a young woman. "A pot that hasn't found its lid", as they say around here. It doesn't seem to worry her, though. Until the arrival of the aid workers she went from one house to another, eating with one family, casting aspersions on another, meddling in other people's lives, an idle existence. She found a purpose with the aid workers, they gave her responsibilities as well as a roof over her head. But the rains came, the drought was over, the aid workers left and Amina is once again at a loose end.

Now the snow has melted, rain has filled the wells and softened the cracked earth, and a thin covering of grass has grown almost everywhere. Grass that breathes with the wind.

It is past midnight when Amina bursts into your room, while you are copying out letters to various bodies, all with the same requests: you ask for books, exercise books, pencils. But no erasers, dried grass does the job perfectly. Letters that you will give to Abdul tomorrow to post in town, letters addressed to *Secours Catholique*, International Red Cross, Emmaus International.

You carry on writing while she stands in front of you talking non-stop. Your silence only makes her more garrulous. She'd thought about it for a long time before deciding not to come today. She can't abide children. The children of Khouf, the children flooding in from the neighbouring villages, all of them nothing but future terrorists and jihadists. Potential killers, ready to come to school with a belt full of explosives around their waist. You'll be blown up along with your class. You're not deaf, you tell her as she yells into your ear that she's going to Noor's, you can meet her there if and when you find your tongue.

Her parting shot is to tell you that it won't be long before your school turns into a pigsty, a trash can with four walls for your so-called pupils who are nothing but scum, a pile of scum. And don't say she didn't warn you.

She brandishes her fist in a gesture of defiance. Is it meant for you or the thunder rumbling above the corrugated metal sheet that passes for a roof?

Amina doesn't like what her life has become. It's like a house without furniture. A house with no windows. She is spinning her wheels, she doesn't know what to do with herself. She was happier when everything rested on her shoulders, when she had to do all the cleaning at the Centre, when she had to battle against the sand that worked its way in under the doors, against cobwebs, ants and scorpions attracted by the cool of the building. When she had to come up with meals to feed the whole team, creating dishes out of nothing, dishes with no name, tasting of nothing, good only for filling the stomach.

22.

The early birds arrive at school soon after cockcrow, night owls, after the call to prayer. Children from the surrounding villages appear later. They present you with an egg, an ear of corn, a chicken wing, payment for your instruction. You divide your charges into three categories: active, hyperactive, and out of control. Noor's sons are the only ones to fall outside all three designations. Zein, Zad, Zahi sleep, faces wedged into their elbows. Should you be concerned? The comatose three are unable to explain themselves and their friends speak on their behalf.

'Working at night.'

'Helping their dad in the casino.'

Three heads nod in approval, eyes closed in sleep beneath long, silky lashes. Eyelashes like their mother's, eyes of the same green. You clap your hands to signal the end of class, and the eyes snap open, startled. Awake, but moody, they deign to tell you what their role is in their father's business. Zahi keeps an eye out for cheaters. Zein vets the would-be players, turns away those who don't pay and the ones whose winnings amount to more than their losses. Zad is the cashier, piling up the dirhams in an old biscuit tin.

You stop the lesson earlier than planned: a bat inside the building has caused panic and sent the fast movers running off, terrorised by the sound of bony wings flapping over their heads, of plaster crumbling from the walls. Lying flat on the ground, the children were surprised to see you standing up, armed with your shoe, flinging it upwards to right and left, missing its target every time.

'Come back tomorrow,' you called to them from the doorway.

You feel disappointed, sad and disappointed. Maybe it would be best to call it a day and close up shop. Today's progress: zero. Conjugating irregular verbs will do nothing to fill the larders. It won't prevent the drought from returning at any moment, it won't stifle the *khamsin* that keeps them imprisoned in their houses like rats, it won't stop the march of the desert that gains ground year after year, crushing houses with its silent footfall, blinding the livestock, stunting the palm trees. You're startled by the sound of laughter, a scornful cackle issuing from the top of the palm tree and running in a stream down the trunk. You look up and see two feet dangling in the air, covered in dirt, cracked as goats' hooves. Amina's voice calls out to you. How did she get herself up there? She says she had no choice, she had to get away from the din made by your pupils, *khafafish*, fools, she calls them. It was her idea, the bat. To get you away from all those donkeys that can't even handle a bale of hay let alone a pencil, pissing in their pants at the sight of a bat. She's said all she had to say and comes down from her perch. The cuts and scrapes she's given herself are of no consequence, they'll heal soon enough with a lick of spit. She decided to park herself up in the tree, as far away as possible from the people of Khouf. She loathes them. The year she's spent among the aid workers has made the scales fall from her eyes. She should be living among the Frenchies, not with the people round here, they're as mad as the *khamsin*, as wretched as their sterile palm trees that don't know whether they're male or female and don't even look like trees, more like upturned brooms from a distance. Amina has hated the people of Khouf for the past five years, ever since she and her mother came seeking refuge after their village was buried under a landslide. They were turned away, sent back towards the desert. 'Let Allah provide food and drink for you,' were the sheikh's words. 'Allah does not forget his children, even those who are undeserving.'

'What happened to your mother?'

She waves her hand in the air, over her shoulder. You take this to mean she is dead.

'Did you have a father?'

She says she did, until the day he burned her with a hot poker because she'd surprised him with a woman, his own brother's wife, while his brother was away from the village. Since that day, everything about love has disgusted her.

Like rutting goats, hens and roosters. The only difference being that billy-goats and roosters look up to heaven and crow with delight or bellow their gratitude to the Creator when they've had their pleasure, but men ask God to forgive them, implore Him to keep Satan at bay and stop him from stealing in at night to impregnate their wives.

Her hatred of men stretches to their children, Noor's most of all. She suspects them of having torn out their mother's door with their own hands. Too much of an effort for Moha, he's much too lazy.

23.

Noor spends all her time tending her plants, watering them morning and night in defiance of the water restrictions imposed by the mayor. She dries them to protect them from catching cold, talks to them, caresses them and promises them she'll leave them as they are for as long as she can, she won't harvest them until she has no other choice. When you talk to her she says nothing, just nods. She hasn't spoken a word to you since Amina put it into her head that she is the heroine of the book you are writing. Noor, the tragic heroine. She wants to be forgotten, her only desire is to see her baby grow. And her vegetables.

In the evenings, when her garden is wrapped in darkness, Noor knits: one row plain, one row pearl. A shapeless form grows beneath her clicking needles, too narrow for a coat, too wide for leggings, too long for a sock. Serene and silent, smiling at the angels only she can see, Noor seems unaware that you and Amina are there. When you ask her a question, all she does is smile, beaming from ear to ear.

Amina concludes that she is bewitched.

'You can cast out the spell, then,' you say.

Amina retorts that she doesn't get mixed up in that kind of thing. Telling fortunes is one thing, but she's not a witch. Curses, spells, leave all that to those who dip their bread in Satan's bowl. Amina is happy to deal with *malaïkas*, with angels, but not with evil spirits, paid under the counter, not declared to the *fisc*.

Hearing her say the word *fisc*, you burst out laughing. Where did she learn the French word for the taxman?

'From Gonzagues,' she confesses. '"No tax to pay so long as I'm doing aid work. Nothing to declare to the *fisc*," he'd say at every turn.'

'Is that all he said to you?'

She blushes and mumbles something about him not talking while he was rubbing himself up against her on Saturdays after the offices had closed and Dr. Paul was taking delivery of medical supplies from the Red Cross and you were at Noor's.

'He needed to get it off his chest, poor guy, or his brain would have exploded along with his groin.'

'He never told you he loved you?'

'Allah preserve us, no!' she replies, sounding offended by the very idea.

Why would he love a dark-skinned woman like her when he has a girlfriend, a woman woven of golden thread, with eyes as blue as the dome of Ali's mosque? Gonzagues was merely relieving himself with Amina, she was doing him a favour, for the sake of his health.

'Why didn't he just find himself a goat?' you ask bitterly.

'Do it with a goat? Outside? No way! You think he'd display his knob for the whole of Khouf to see?'

She chides you for your lack of understanding. Says you have become as hard as the people of Khouf. Turned to stone, with a heart of stone. How does she know? Because you didn't consummate your marriage with Abdul.

Amina's words pour forth, like flames searing your closed eyelids. Exhausted from another day's work you make no effort to set her right on the subject of Abdul. Your thoughts are of Gonzagues abusing this woman's trust, subjugating her to his every whim. Memories come back to you, fragments, cracked images. You hear his voice ordering Amina to mop under his shoes, making no effort to lift his feet from the ground. A cocky young man of twenty-five, barely concealing his scorn for the forty-year old woman. Derisive, imperious, delighting in seeing her on all fours in front of him. The humanitarian veneer cracking to reveal the colonial beneath.

Amina went off the rails after he left. She could have helped you keep order in the class, but she deserted the Centre. The once so sensible woman has become a shadow of her former self. She wanders around the central square, makes forays into the shop, buys a bottle of alcohol, the same every time, drinks it in one gulp and staggers off like a ship in a storm. Yesterday she started talking to a tree, thinking it was a friend of hers. Then she banged her forehead against a donkey's head, thought it was the barber and told it to do a better job of shaving next time. When she realised it was a donkey she proceeded to curse the tree, the donkey, the barber and the people standing around laughing their heads off at her.

Driven mad by love, by humiliation, Amina stamps her foot and declares that it was there, over the basin, and nowhere else that Gonzagues "defenestrated" her. An odd expression on the lips of a woman who doesn't even have a house of her own, let alone a window.

You tell her you hope she comes back next time as a tortoise, that way she'll have her own house.

'There you go again,' she says. 'That's exactly what I'm talking about. Amina knows how to give. But you have a heart of stone, your garden is all rocks.'

Seeing your dazed expression, she deigns to explain what she means.

She berates you for your indifference towards the men who love you. You never replied to your French lover's letters, you didn't consummate your marriage with Abdul.

She is being disingenuous, you think, and remind her that it was a marriage for form's sake only, to enable you to plead Noor's cause before the mullah and the minister. But Amina sees the matter in a different light. A marriage, she says, is a marriage, a bond between adults. Not some game played in a pretend school with thugs masquerading as pupils, an old warehouse dressed up as a classroom for idiots who pretend to learn and go away with their heads even emptier than they were to start with. A real school mistress, she declares, is a mother too. She teaches her children while she is cooking. Serves letters of the alphabet with her meatballs. A proper school mistress should be married, with a man in her bed. She passes on to her pupils the gifts he bestows on her: tenderness, kind words, caresses.

Powerless to counter her attacks, you burst into tears and Amina immediately melts.

Like the parched earth of Khouf, Amina needs water to soften her hard edges. Your tears propel her into your embrace, where she weeps, her loneliness flowing into yours. For you are alone, as alone as she is, as the moon among the stars, as solitary as Noor's goat condemned to graze in isolation. Alone and unashamed, choking on your pride. All you have taken from your marriage with good, kind Abdul, is the veneer, the aroma. In other words, nothing. Well, if you're not going to eat the shish kebabs, concludes Amina, you might as well enjoy the smell. And yet Gonzagues didn't leave her anything of his, not even one of his handkerchiefs. No notes or letters either, since the only language he speaks is French. She is poor in memories, poor in words. The poorest of the poor, queen of the beggars. He'd promised to help her find work in France, she'd have been happy with anything.

She was expecting a letter. When he sent her a postcard, it was an aerial view of Paris with an arrow pointing to a building. His home.

24.

Evenings with the three of you have settled in to a routine. Amina mopes. Noor knits and you wring your hands, unable to find the words to reassure Amina of your friendship, incapable of making Noor understand that the shape growing beneath her needles looks nothing like a baby's coat, bears no resemblance to either leggings or socks.

Amina's sulks are punctuated with sobs and disconnected words which you try to put together into sentences.

She seems to be saying that you and Noor are the only family she has. Her sisters in sorrow. Her chest resonates like a gong beneath her fist. Amina has purged her life of love. The only man who ever paid attention to her has cut out half of her heart. The other half is only fit to be thrown to the dogs.

She gestures towards her heart, mimes tearing it out and throwing it on the ground.

Once her tears have dried and her heart has been restored to her breast, she declares that she has no regrets.

The pounding she took from Gonzagues made her feel like Marilyn Monroe.

She has no regrets, and no expectations. Women in Paris are as numerous as the stars in the sky. And what chance would she have, with her short legs, against all those girls with legs as long as palm trees?

Noor goes on counting stitches, her composure unruffled.

Her voice, when she calls Zad, Zein, Zahi from her doorway, has lost the intensity it once had. She calls them once, and leaves it at that, certain they will not oppose their father's wishes. As her belly grows rounder, she calls them with less conviction, while the unborn child, the baby she once wanted only to be rid of, grows to fill the space between her hips.

Does she know that Zahi, Zad, Zein come to your school? She never asks you, only fixes you with her questioning sea-blue gaze.

You look away, unable to meet her eyes, leaving her alone with her imaginings. Noor never mentions the girl in the village who was raped by the man in the jeep. Cut off as she is from village life, has she heard about the headache the girl's case has created for the mayor and the qadi? And for the sheikh who gave the aggrieved parents permission to have their daughter sewn up so they could find a taker for her once her hymen was restored?

The girl's case is on everyone's lips, even your pupils are talking about it. Fascinated and repulsed, they wonder if the man in the jeep penetrated Zana in the same way as their fathers do their mothers: the man on top, the woman underneath. Or did he do it like dogs and bitches do, like billy-goats and nannies, donkeys and jennies? The female held beween the front legs, the male standing upright pumping away frantically?

The violent wind that blew that night in Khouf adds to the confusion. As violent as the *khamsin*, icy-cold and biting. Birds fell from the sky, hard as stones, rigid, their skin tinged with blue, their beaks open in one long screech. The few people to venture out that night threw themselves on the ground, tumbling and rolling, their *djellabas* billowing in the wind.

From a distance, they looked like barrels.

How is it possible that Zana's father sent his daughter out to fetch water on such a night? And from a well that was dry?

Her father dragged her to the Centre, calling for vengeance, her mother beating herself, tearing at her chest. Dr. Paul accepted their story, not doubting the truth of their accusation. Moved by their predicament, he promised to do what he could to help them.

Your students can't take their eyes off Zana, who sits at the back of the class, seemingly unaware of them. She stares over their heads, her eyes fixed on your lips, her thirst for knowledge greater than theirs. She hangs on your every word, writes everything down in the notebook her father gave her. She writes from right to left, from left to right, each word written once in Arabic, once in French, side by side. Alif next to A, ba' beside B, kaf with K, tah and T, dal and D all the way to Z; she does the rest during break. With her swelling belly, she can't go out and run around. Your heart goes out to her, but she seems unaffected by her plight, shows no signs of unhappiness. Like Noor, she accepts her fate. The women of Khouf have expunged self-pity from their vocabulary. Like donkeys loaded with back-breaking burdens, they walk blindly ahead, never faltering from the path, commanding respect.

Zana writes with one hand, the other resting on her belly as if to protect it. She must love this child that has brought shame on the family. The sight of Zana making the same pregnant woman's gesture as Noor moves you, makes you throw caution to the wind. You decide to ask her what name she will give the child.

'His father's,' she replies, blurting out the answer without a moment's hesitation.

Her mother will raise the child; he'll be her little brother. They have the same father anyway.

She is the first to register surprise at what she has just revealed. She has inadvertently confided in you, it's too late to retract what she said.

'What does your mother think of what's happened to you?'

'My mother doesn't think, my mother weeps and wails. She says no man will marry a girl who's not intact, that it's pointless to have me sewn up before the baby comes.

Apparently you can be made as good as new for two hundred dirhams.'

So much for the naïve child you thought her to be, she turns out to be wily, prepared to resort to any trick to find a taker.

Overcome by a wave of nausea mixed with pity, you rush outside and vomit repeatedly beneath the palm tree. Children gaze at you with worried faces, interrupting their games to stare at you. Is the teacher ill? Seriously ill? The teacher had better not die here in Khouf, there would be nowhere to bury her.

No sooner have they surrounded you than they scatter once more. Their concern is fleeting, no more lasting than their careless indifference. They're on their way home. Any excuse to avoid studying, a bat in the classroom, their teacher feeling a little unwell. They only come to school if their parents force them to.

When the others have gone, Zana, who has been sitting down all this time, stands up and heads for the door, her stomach now clearly visible.

'I'm five months gone,' she informs you even though you have not asked.

Five months pregnant, and it's scarcely a month since the night of the snowstorm, the night she was supposedly raped.

25.

The children have gone home when Amina bursts in to
the classroom to warn you not to persist in trying to teach
them to read and write, especially the girls who would
be better off spending their time sewing and knitting. A
woman does not need to be able to read. A woman reads
desire in a man's eyes, kindles her flame in response to the
fire in the hearth, kneads her belly and the unrisen dough
with one movement. What need is there of reading in
this village where there is only one book to be found, the
sheikh's. Reading and writing are for city dwellers, not for
people who live here on the edge of the desert. Words are
erased here by the sand whipped up by rival winds. Letters
don't get delivered here. The postman is illiterate, he can't
read the addresses on the envelopes, he can't see his route
for the drifting sand. Letters end up returned to sender.
The postman had nothing to do and now he's retired. He
swapped his bicycle for a donkey, and now he spends his
days counting his prayer beads from morning to night.

Going to the mosque gives him something to do. Amina stares into your eyes and tells you how worried she is about your fiancé, as she calls him.

'It's a bad sign, his silence. He hasn't written to you in over six months. He could be dead. Hanged from a fig tree.'

'Why a fig tree?' you ask, unable to hide your irritation.

'A fig tree, a palm tree, makes no difference,' she says, sounding annoyed. 'The important thing is that I can see him dangling from a branch, on the end of a rope.'

Desperate for you to share in her visions, Amina is becoming ever more unhinged. She says angels are speaking through her. They talk to her, but only when she is perched atop the palm tree, never when she is on solid ground. Up there she feels as high as the muezzin in his minaret, high above the people of Khouf who have always despised her.

Is it pride or madness?

Amina would never have talked like this when the aid workers were here. Their departure turned her head upside down. No more Gonzagues to submit to, as a slave to her master, no more employer to pay her wages, so meagre they weighed no more than a grasshopper's wing. You decide to test her visionary powers and ask her to tell you what has become of the man who violated Noor the night of the *khamsin*.

'Dead!' she exclaims categorically.

'And what of Zad, Zahi, Zein? They've stopped coming to school.'

'Dead too.'

'And what will happen to Noor?'

'She'll die by the stones, crushed, finished for good.'

You remind her that the mullah responsible for virtue gave you to believe there was hope for her.

Amina is unconvinced.

'What is a mullah in the face of an earthquake? Khouf will be wiped from the face of the earth, sand upon sand, a battleground for brambles, home of the winds. Khouf will be swallowed up under the water when the dam is built. Drowned, along with its mosque, its sheikh and all its inhabitants. The first to go will be the walls, weary of housing liars and layabouts.'

You retaliate and describe the joy on your pupils' faces when they discovered that their words for car, taxi and bus were the same in French.

'Words for things on wheels,' she replies haughtily. 'Not for the food we eat. Real food, not the hamburgers you people eat all the time.'

No point in trying to argue with her. Since she's been up in the tree, she's become all-knowing. From her palm tree she can see what goes on in people's heads. Empty, all of them, skulls where the *khamsin* has made its bed. They only hear what they want to hear, their tongues repeat the same things they've been saying since the beginning of time. Donkeys. All of them, donkeys. Even the wind avoids them, swerving off in a different direction when it comes up against them, stifling itself.

Odd that she still spends all her time with these people she claims to despise.

For some time now Amina has been overwhelmed with requests. People come from all around to consult her, from Khouf as well as neighbouring villages. No one dares counter her predictions, not even Moha. He still swears by her even though she predicted he would find wealth and success and he's been bankrupted by his mounting debts.

News of his casino closing down came as a hammer blow to the regular gamblers. Now that Moha has put the key back under the mat and made off with the last of the takings, they have nowhere to spend their evenings.

Noor stands in her doorway and asks if anyone has seen Zahi, Zad, Zein.

As if the doorstep could give her an answer. But it remains silent, waiting for someone to cross Noor's threshold. The door has nothing to say either, and nor does the key.

An individual who's scarcely to be trusted claims to have seen them running towards the desert, backwards. Why backwards, the qadi asked, ever the pragmatist.

Because they've always done everything in reverse, from the moment they were born. Noor knitted their jackets the wrong way round so they could wear them the right way. Zahi, Zad, Zein: doing everything with their left hand. Not that they'd ever held anything resembling a pen or a pencil. Left-handed and left-footed. Left foot in the right sock, right foot in the left sock. Walking like a clock stopped at ten past ten.

With Moha's house under seal, Zahi, Zein, Zad put an end to their aimless wanderings in the desert. They come to their senses and remember they have a mother. They make their way to her house, bringing the door they snatched from under the nose of a bailiff while he was making a list of Moha's remaining possessions: four mats and four bowls. No need for Noor to open her door for them, they are carrying it on their shoulders. She scrutinises them as they return her gaze and starts jumping up and down around them, like a dog, overjoyed to be reunited with its master. Zad, Zahi, Zein seem happy to be back with their mother, in spite of the change in her. She is rounder, much rounder and acting strangely, knitting peculiar things she calls sweaters even though her creations have no opening for a head. No, she is knitting sweaters, she insists. She has taken up speaking again, but only in their presence, not with you. She suspects you more than ever of wanting to put her in the book you are writing, choking at the thought of being enclosed between the covers.

You know better than most, how much Noor hates to be shut in.

You leave her alone with her happiness and rely on Amina to keep you updated, Amina who doesn't understand why Noor is besotted with three ignorant, treacherous ingrates.

'Have you heard how she talks to them now?' she asks

you, beside herself with rage.

Without waiting for an answer she tells you she's worried that Noor seems to be confusing her sons with her plants. She calls Zahi her courgette flower, Zein her heart's tomato, and Zad her beloved basil plant.

Your sleepless nights are spent in a confusion of thoughts. Was Noor already mad when you first met her? Her refusal to accuse the man who raped her; her stubborn determination to accept her sentence as just, claiming that the stranger had given her pleasure; not objecting to Moha's theft of her door on the grounds that he paid for it. Were these all signs of courage and dignity, or symptoms of a deranged mind? And now you're saddled with with two crackpot friends, the two mad women of the village. Each as unhinged as the other, one delivering her ravings from the top of a tree, the other on solid ground.

Amina and Noor have shed their skin, like snakes, sloughing off their old selves and taking on new ones: the cleaning woman from the Centre has transformed into an oracle, the fallen woman has become the model mother of three, with a fourth soon to come. When you arrived in Khouf, they didn't know what to make of you. They couldn't understand why you had travelled across so many countries to forget a man and a cat. Do they have more time for you now that you've become the school teacher in a village of illiterates? You are determined to teach them to write. You have plenty of time. Your days are packed, your nights crowded with wakefulness. Your life is filled with crumbs from the lives of others. You go to bed with the chickens and wake as the cock crows. At the end of each day, alone in the warehouse that passes for a school, you look at the blackboard pinned to the wall, the bits of chalk scattered around on the mats that the goats would eat if you didn't go round picking them up. When night falls, you feel as old as the mountains and the desert. Khouf has aged you a thousand years.

26.

Lying in bed, waiting for sleep to come, you listen to the sand grating against the shutters. If it weren't for the window panes, the desert would have seeped into your room and into your bed. Between the slats of the shutter, the moon appears to be sitting in Amina's place, perched atop the palm tree, while she sleeps in the warehouse. The moon was never this big in Paris, it's almost as if two moons exist, one small and flat, for the west, and another, immense and rounded, for the east. Camel drivers gaze up at it, wondering if their loved ones will recognise them after so many months away. Noor calls it the powder puff moon. Noor, in her eighth month of pregnancy, blooming since she was reunited with her sons. The sheikh says the moon is the light of the Prophet Muhammad. It is the only light in Khouf tonight. The *douar* is wrapped in darkness. No lights flicker in the windows.

All of a sudden, you see flames rise up from the direction of Noor's house, leaping towards the sky, engulfing the village in smoke. Brutally roused from their slumber, people go rushing towards the flames with buckets of water, voices call out, shout, curse. You watch from your window, as Noor forbids them to come near her hedge. She tells them she is free to reduce her belongings to ashes if she chooses to, free to feed her trunk, her two window-frames, her chair, her camel-hair blanket and even her cooking-pot to the fire.

No one dares approach. Everyone knows the devil lurks beneath the skin of the insane. When she can find nothing else to cast into the flames, Noor takes off her dress, slipping it over her head and throwing it into the fire along with the rest. She stands naked behind the flames, utterly naked. Women mumble *ta'wizat*, men feast their eyes, children snigger. Violence takes hold. Mothers thrash their children, throwing them to the ground. Two men grapple with each other for no apparent reason, a donkey bites a goat, another goat eats its way through an entire thicket, dogs howl at the moon which, at the sight of the naked pregnant woman, hides behind a scrap of cloud.

Someone knocks at your door, pulls you outside. People say you are the only one capable of reasoning with Noor. As soon as you cross the line of the hedge she throws herself against your chest and sobs her heart out. With a despairing gesture she points to her uprooted plants, piled up in a corner. It was Moha who killed them. When he came back from his wanderings and found his sons weren't at his house, he lashed out at their mother.

Noor had resigned herself to everything, even to the idea of dying under a hail of stones from her kin. But the attack on her courgettes, her tomatoes and aubergines is too much to bear. Without her garden, she cannot go on living.

27.

The aid-workers' Centre has become a temporary shelter, a refuge for those in need. At night, mats and mattresses are unrolled on the ground for the pupils who come from distant *douars* and only go back home at weekends. They sleep head to toe, like kings and queens in a pack of cards, cook their own meals in a pot balanced on three stones over a fire of brushwood. Once the lamp is blown out, everyone sleeps, except for Noor and Amina who sit and talk, sometimes until dawn, arguing occasionally when the conversation turns to comparisons between Gonzagues and the stranger in the jeep, favouring one and not the other. Exhausted from teaching, you don't join in, preferring to follow their conversation from the other side of the wall. Their talk makes you think of your lover and you imagine yourself back in Paris, standing in front of your building. You see yourself putting your key in the lock and opening the door as the phone rings insistently. You recognise him from his breathing. Then you hear, 'I'm coming' whispered

into the phone. You turn round, not knowing how to prepare for him, you start by opening the curtains to let light
into the room. The grass has grown more thickly over your
cat's grave than elsewhere, a flower grows on it, a blossom
of five petals, standing guard, a fragile, fleeting headstone
at the mercy of smallest breath of wind. Nothing is per-
manent. You expect nothing from his return, nothing from
yourself. Grass has grown over your hearts just as it has
over the grave you dug with your own hands eight months
earlier.

A waking dream, suppressed before it can take hold.
You've accepted your defeat, unlike your two friends who
are sucked further into their delusions. Noor stares at the
road all night long hoping to see a jeep appear. Amina goes
to the bus stop every evening, convinced that Abdul will
bring her a letter from Gonzagues. She strides through the
village with a determined step, looking for all the world
as if she is going to meet someone who is waiting for her.
Gonzagues was the final straw for her capricious mind. She
goes a little madder every day. No longer the humble fortune-teller, content to read the coffee grounds in exchange
for a handful of dates or a plate of *chorba*, Amina's taken to
believing she has the ear of spirits from the higher realms
of the universe.

She claims the Prophet has appeared to her, sitting on
a flying carpet. He called her by name and ordered her
to inform the sheikh that he had thought long and hard

about the problem of Noor and decided to declare her innocent. And therefore she will not be stoned, but can return immediately to Moha's house, even though Moha has been homeless since the bailiff put the seals on his house and forbade him to cross the threshold. If you tell her that she dreamt it all, the Prophet, the flying carpet, everything, she retorts that she never dreams, she's too poor for such luxuries. The people of Khouf laugh behind her back. Dogs seem to be her only friends. They sniff her respectfully, never bite her. Some of them even bring her half-chewed scraps. Nothing but marrow and bone.

The light has been blown out, everyone but your two friends is asleep. Noor has no memory of the night she laid waste to her humble home. But her eyes have not forgotten. She only has to blink and flames rise up before her. Dawn was breaking over the mountain when you took her back to your place. A woman took pity on her and tossed you an *abaya* to cover her, another woman spat in her face. Noor was shaking with pent-up anger and from the cold night air that descends on the desert after the heat of the day has dissipated. Her head tucked under your arm, she seemed smaller than ever, unless it was sadness that had shrunk her. She'd pass unnoticed if it weren't for her prominent belly buffeted by the kicks and punches of the child in her womb. Mother and child fired by the same furious intensity.

Noor, a jug of milk filled to overflowing, a river of mud

that's burst its banks, a saucepan that's boiled over. Noor, the black widow spider who weaves her web and then destroys it.

The devil has entered her through her opened crack, says the sheikh, a devil that can only be expelled by the stones piled up in the square. He doubts the authenticity of the document signed by the mullah. The foreign woman falsified it. She never met the holy man. The city is too far away from Khouf for anyone to confirm she met him.

Noor pays no attention to the rumours. She is cut off from everything, except the road she scrutinises day and night. Will it bring her the man in the jeep, or executioners bearing stones?

A black cloud fills her eyes as she scans the scorched patch of earth enclosed by the cactus hedge. You try to offer her words of comfort. You tell her the wind will ensure her aubergines, courgettes, tomatoes and basil plant are carried off to kinder ground, far away from the desert, but she shakes her head.

'Better to spare the wind and not try to save the plants,' she says. 'They were murdered, they'll be full of bitterness even if they're transplanted somewhere else.'

You remind her that she has something worth much more than a vegetable plot and a mean little house. She is going to have a child.

'Children,' she retorts. 'Like the moon. Beautiful from a distance.'

'You should stop hoping for the man in the jeep to

return,' you say. 'He might have gone back to his country.'

'A man is not a tree,' she replies. 'He walks, goes from place to place. One day he's here, another day he's somewhere else. You just have to wait.'

You tell her that her sons have decided to rebuild her burnt-out house, and she says she's happy to hear that Zahi, Zad, Zein, who've never been able to string two words together, at least know how to pile stones on top of one another.

Amina is worried for Noor. She's convinced she won't live much longer than her vegetable garden. She pronounces the sentence with all the authority of a doctor listening to the final spasms of a dying heart. Has the young medic's scientific language rubbed off on her? Yesterday she announced that an earthquake was imminent. 'A seismic tremor,' she said, declaiming with eyes glazed, staring off into the distance. 'Caused by the impact of two tectonic plates colliding and rupturing the earth's crust, after which there will be flooding.' Amina, the visionary. The gift of clairvoyance bestowed on her through suffering.

28.

Zahi, Zein, Zad disappear every morning and come back at nightfall, their hands stiff from kneading mud and straw into a smooth paste to rebuild their house.

Muted sounds from the building site reach their mother's ears: spades scraping, wood being trimmed for windows and door. She doesn't bat an eyelid. Her attention is focused entirely on the road. Surely the jeep will appear at any moment. She knows it, instinctively. An unseen hand has drawn a line from the embrace in the eye of the *khamsin* to the birth of the child, expected any day now.

A black shape approaches, a local man. The sheikh. Noor recognises his turban. His huge form grows in size as he draws closer, blotting out the sun and turning day into night. She is seized with dread, paralysed. She cannot flee. Invisible nails pin her to the doorstep. He pretends not to see her, addresses his words to the air, to the palm tree. Then, he spins around and declares that her sentence was not commuted, merely adjourned. She will be stoned as planned, but after the birth of the child. This is what the mullah's letter meant, she must be ready to meet her Maker.

The sheikh seems to be losing his mind. Yesterday the mullah's letter didn't exist, now it is a reality.

Noor says nothing in response. She stands, like a statue while the sheikh, tired after walking from one end of the *douar* to the other, squats at the foot of the palm tree, facing her. She forgets to breathe, to blink. A family of swallows nesting in the tree perch in a line along a branch and launch into furious squawking, as if to wrench Noor from her stupor. The sheikh stands up, driven to distraction by the screeching and the droppings raining down on him. He brandishes his cane to left and right, hitting out at random, unable to find a target. Composing himself, he reins in his anger and recites a verse in an effort to restore his dignity:

"Those who stray from the path will receive no guidance. He turns from them in their transgression, and leaves them confounded and faltering."

Seeing that the holy words have no effect on Noor, he continues with a second verse, his voice thundering, loud enough to shatter glass.

"Allah accepts only the repentance of those who commit evil in ignorance and repent until the angel of death appears at their bedside. Allah is all-knowing and wise."

He looks her in the eye and asks her to admit that she experienced pleasure with the stranger, that she committed adultery in full knowledge of what she was doing.

'Confess, woman.'

Weary of talking to a lifeless statue, the sheikh mops his brow and recites a third verse, more pointed this time.

"If any of your women commit fornication, call in four witnesses among yourselves. If they testify to her guilt, confine her in your house until death overtakes her or until Allah decrees another fate for her."

The sheikh cites three witnesses, counting them on his fingers: Zahi, Zad, Zein. He stares off into space, trying to think of a fourth.

Seeing Amina loom into view behind Noor, he names the cat that perished the night of the *khamsin*, saying it would have survived if Noor had gone on searching instead of lying with the stranger.

'An animal can't be a witness,' Amina retorts.

'And neither can a witch,' he counters, 'a witch like you, and the woman sheltering you.' He turns and looks towards your office, trying to glimpse you behind the window. 'A woman travelling alone is cause for suspicion. She sleeps alone so she can welcome Satan into her bed. She claims she is teaching our children to read and write, but in reality, she is turning them against my teachings. Only the *madrasa* can raise them out of their ignorance, teach them not to steal and lie.'

A sound that he takes for applause hailing his long speech comes from the top of the palm tree, from the swallows, paying him no attention as they shake out their feathers in one shared movement and prepare to fly away.

29.

Dawn's first glow touches the slats of your blinds. The sun's rays sweep across the desert, illuminating the morning mist as it creeps along the ground, suffusing the clouds that float overhead with light. You wake up in your bed, out of a dream. Somewhere, far away from here, you were standing on a sheet of ice knocking at the door of a mud brick house, but no one answered. Zana's voice called out, telling you to throw a stone at the window, to break the glass and rouse the people within.

'What stone?' you asked, unable to see any around you.

'The stone in my frozen heart,' she snapped, as if the answer were obvious.

'Where are you, Zana?' you asked. 'Why have you stopped coming to school? Are you ill?'

'Ask my father. He's the only one who has the right to answer for me. He's always spoken for me. My death won't change anything.'

Thank God, it's just a dream, you think as you leap out bed, in a hurry to get out of your room and go outside. The fresh air will blow away the nightmare.

When you arrive at your school, you find a girl waiting for you outside, the first to arrive. She stares at you from behind her long thick eyelashes. A curtain of black silk. You ask her if she knows where Zana's house is and she turns points to a run-down mud house next to the mosque, indistinguishable from all the others. You follow her directions, in spite of your fear of confronting Zana's father once again. Waste ground, faded time-worn hovels. Women squatting over their fires stare at you above their cooking pots as you pass by. 'What wind has brought the foreign woman here to the poorest part of Khouf ?' their eyes seem to say.

You find the house, bang on the door and are greeted with the sound of an iron bar being removed. From behind the half-open door a voice orders you to go away. No one wants to talk to you. You insist. You have a book to give to Zana.

'My daughter has no use for your book, she can't read.'

The answer hits you like a slap in the face. Your cheek burns. The door slams violently shut, the metal bar clangs back into place, like a stone crashing down on a tomb.

You would have gone back the next day but that same evening you hear shouts coming from that part of the *douar*. You join the crowd of people running towards the house next to the mosque, everyone in Khouf wondering what is going on. Zana's mother shouts:

'I'm next, am I? First you murder your daughter, then me?'

An accusation hurled into the night, into the silence, thrown to the wind going from door to door, alerting everyone in Khouf.

'He's cut her throat. He's thrown her into the well with no shroud, no prayers, no *fatiha*. Like a dog.'

Now that she has spoken, nothing can stop the flow of her words.

'He killed her, and the child he was father to.'

When the water carrier came to remove the body he found nothing but a skeleton stripped of its flesh. The rattling of Zana's bones sounded like bells tinkling.

Back at the Centre, you weep for the girl who longed to read and write. She would have succeeded had it not been for her abusive father. The theory of the stranger driving the jeep is no longer tenable. It was her father who killed her, but he will not be brought to justice. Neither the sheikh nor the qadi will act. His daughter's life was his to dispose of as he pleased.

30.

Noor scratches at your door, certain you're not asleep. She's been kept awake by news of the discovery of Zana's body. No one had even noticed she'd disappeared. She's afraid she will suffer the same fate and doesn't know how she could stop someone from slitting her throat. Light from her lamp illuminates the bookcase with its rows of books, your own and those left by your predecessors at the Centre. She doesn't understand why you keep them. Might as well hang on to your old clothes. But the map on the wall intrigues her.

She asks you what it all means. You explain that it shows where each country is. Green is for forests, grey for mountains, ochre for the desert and blue for the sea. She asks where Khouf is and is disappointed to see it's a nothing but a dot. Forty houses, the grocery shop, the mosque and the brickworks all reduced to a dot.

'And the dam?'

You point to the river.

'I want to see the dam,' she insists.

'It's not marked. Not until they've finished building it.'

Hands on her hips in a defiant stance, she asks you why you say "they" when you know that he's building it by himself.

As far as Noor is concerned, the map is all wrong. She won't be swayed by a piece of paper, she can't be expected to believe that the dam is no further than a finger's width away from Khouf.

Whatever the map says, she intends to go there. The man in the jeep will be happy to see her. Cutthroats won't come looking for her that far away.

You remind her that he's left the country, that they stopped work on the dam when they ran out of funds. And in her advanced state of pregnancy, walking fifteen kilometres won't be so easy.

She goes quiet, turns her pale face towards you. Will she really go in search of the man whose child she is carrying? You find it hard to believe she will.

A door slams shut, footsteps trail off into the night. Her retreating figure looks like the shadow of a palm tree.

Too tired to think, you huddle down under the covers and sink into sleep. You dream you're getting married to Abdul's brother. A boy with a future, the people around you exclaim admiringly. A slaughterer. A self-made man. Your future husband depends on nothing but the knife he keeps sharpened and ready, unlike Abdul who doesn't even own his own bus. Jabbar, his name is, he's educated, studied for a whole year at the Qur'anic school. He has a powerful voice, he could be a muezzin. Slaughterer and muezzin. Not just one job, but two.

The ceremony unfolds. No one has asked what you think. You want to escape but you're surrounded by old women ululating, heads thrown back. The sheikh doesn't take his eyes off you. He isn't convinced by your conversion, he conducted it warily. Your name will be Noor, he declared as he tore up your passport and reduced your French name to dust.

Noor.

People crowd around you, *hennayats* etch designs deeply into your palms, a stray lock of hair is hurriedly hidden under the veil that covers you from head to foot. Smells of rosewater, jasmine blossom, musk and cloves. Surrounded by faces glowing with joy, you're the only one who's not happy. You want to leave but don't know which way to go, the map on the wall over your bookshelf is all wrong, Khouf has been cut off by a landslide. Your letters to aid agencies asking for textbooks, notebooks, pencils have not been sent. No post has arrived. As far as the west is concerned you are in a war zone. But the conflict has been going on for decades and the country is held in the grip of a drought more murderous than any war.

You wake up, relieved to hear the wind tearing at your shutters, trying to pull them off their hinges, putting an end to the nightmare. Your name is not Noor, no one has confiscated your passport. You are free to leave, to go back home to the small world of your flat, your garden and your job, to find a new cat, a new lover even.

'And what would become of Noor?' you ask out loud.

Amina brings her worries with your morning coffee. Today's fears are bleaker than the bitter brew, darker than the grounds in which she reads the future.

She sees Noor scaling a mountain, falling into a crevasse, mustering all her strength to haul herself out, encountering a snake, a river in flood, clinging to a branch in the river and washing up on the other shore outside a locked house. She calls out but no one answers. She hammers on the door with her fists but no one opens up. She is exhausted, her waters break, she squats and gives birth to a stillborn child.

'Your cup, foreign woman, spills over with tears,' she concludes in a desolate voice.

Amina was supposed to be your assistant, but she's never set foot in your classroom. The children suck the air from her lungs, fill her head with noise, scare away her benevolent spirits, the ones who protect her and reveal her visions to her. Standing in front the children of Khouf, Amina feels as empty as a nut forgotten by the summer.

Perhaps she's right.

A day of unending disappointments.

The earth is round, you tell the children, it turns in space. They don't disagree, but point out that round or not, it's still flat, as flat as a plate, the stars and the sun are above and there's nothing below, otherwise houses would fall into valleys, fields would slide into rivers and men would spin like tops instead of walking.

'The earth is fixed to the ground.'

You show them the five continents on the map: Europe where you used to live, Asia where they are now, then Paris where you were before you came to Khouf. 'By donkey?' they ask in unison, for they know that planes bring only soldiers. They see them flying over like eagles. Flying over the desert on their way to bomb the mujaheddin in the mountains.

'Is there a desert in Paris?' the bright spark asks.

'Does Paris have a mosque?'

'Does the moon in Paris tell you when it's Ramadan?' someone asks anxiously.

The question from the one who shouts loudest is the one you answer first. Of course people celebrate Ramadan in Paris. And Christmas too. Streets are festooned with lights and decorations. Children wait excitedly for Father Christmas to bring them presents, he has gifts for everyone, even for naughty children.

You draw Father Christmas on the board, but no one shows much enthusiasm. You give him a moustache and a beard as a finishing touch anyway.

'Your Father Christmas looks just like the sheikh.'

A little voice pipes up from the back of the class asking if Papa Christmas has four wives and lots of children too, if he dines on stuffed lamb and chicken every day.

The question is greeted with a scathing laugh from the wearer of the Bin Laden tee-shirt, the image life-size and mocking.

Why should Father Christmas matter any more than the Minister for Suppression of Vice, or the mullah charged with protecting virtue? He's nothing but a western invention, a way of showing that old people get all the food they want in the west.

One last question throws you into confusion.

'Do children in Paris stand on the roof and call up to the moon at New Year?

The sky suddenly turns dark and you are spared from answering the question. The children must hurry home before it starts to rain. Just the excuse they've been waiting for. As you watch Rahim climb on his donkey, you realise he's the only one who can give you news of the man in the jeep. Has he come back from his trip? Have the works started up again? And Noor, has she gone looking for him? Did Rahim see her on his way to school? A pregnant woman is hard to miss.

After the children have gone, you linger in the doorway, delighting in the spectacle of the view spread out before your eyes. The earth, so parched and cracked when you arrived in Khouf, is now covered in luxuriant growth, its yellow, ochre and chalky hues replaced by every shade of green. Golden green for the wheat swaying in the wind, darker green for the alfalfa creeping close to the ground, while the maize planted at the edge of the desert glints green and grey.

Khouf will no longer be hungry or thirsty, rain and snowmelt have filled the wells, irrigated the fields. The water table is replenished. Now all that's needed to make it flow is some digging.

You think of Noor who left two days ago, of her mattress unslept on in the warehouse, of her sons working on her house for a good while now with no visible results.

When she told you she was leaving, you didn't believe her. A pregnant woman cannot climb a mountain or cross a river. Like a cat she concentrates all her energy on the fruit ripening in her womb, she forgets about the male.

Amina signals to you, waving her arms in the air. She has news for you, good and bad. The good news is that a box is going to be delivered to you later in the day. From Paris, it must be the books and school supplies you asked *Secours Catholique* for. The bad news is that she can't find Noor. For all she knows, she's gone back to Moha and he's hidden her away until she drops her brat so he can drown it the way he used to drown the cats she collected.

You only half believe her. Amina is no more to be trusted than your dreams. The earthquake that cut Khouf off from the rest of the country never happened, the postman is still delivering post, he has a parcel for you. That leaves Noor. Is it possible that she's gone back to Moha? Thrown herself into the lion's den, delivered herself to her executioner with hands and feet bound? Driven by worry, you go out into the street. You ask passers-by, the two shopkeepers. The grocer, who sells nothing but candles, rope and can-openers remembers seeing her walking by, but he's not sure in which direction. The barber, an Islamist of the first order, refuses to look at women. Old Jalila is the only one who says she's seen Noor. She was heading for her house. Now that her sons have repaired the façade and filled all the holes, there's no reason for her to live anywhere else.

Zahi, Zad, Zein are pretending to work and haven't seen their mother for two days. Their so-called building works advance at snail's pace, with the builders more likely to be seen on the roof, basking in the sun, than working on the outside of the house.

The butcher, who likes to stir up gossip, says people would have seen her if she'd gone back home. There's no mistaking a mother, even one who opened her flower to a stranger.

The next day, Rahim announces to general amazement that he's seen a woman struggling up the hill towards the dam.

'A pregnant woman?'

Rahim is embarrassed and reluctant to commit himself. All he will say is that she was well-rounded, all over, he didn't look under her robes.

'As if she'd show him her nest,' Jalila sneers, pointing lewdly between her thighs.

Her gesture reminds you of an odd incident. You saw Noor cooking up a sugary paste on a hotplate the night before she vanished. It smelled sweet, like a caramel dessert.

'A craving?'

She nodded her head, both ways, both yes and no. It was Amina with her suspicious mind who'd explained to you that what you thought was caramel was sugar wax. Noor was preparing herself for a man. Preparing herself to be penetrated.

After dark, you saw her peering at the mountain, at the cliffs that conceal the site of the dam.

Noor has put all her trust in her instinct, and in your map. If she'd known that Rahim lived near the site of the dam she'd have asked him, but she's never come across the boy on his donkey. Since being excluded from the life of the *douar*, Noor has seen no one but you and Amina, she hasn't spoken to anyone else. The women who brought her their left-overs and their dirty laundry didn't speak to her, they just put their bundle on the ground by the cactus hedge and came to collect it in the evening from the same spot – the plate licked clean and the clothes laundered. Noor has no friends, it's common knowledge. Those few who took pity on her when she was first condemned have joined the ranks of her enemies since she set fire to her house.

Like a goat shaken free of her tether, Noor has capered off over the mountain to see if the grass is greener on the other side.

31.

Noor walks, her gaze fixed on the top of the mountain. The invisible line drawn between her eyes and the snow-capped peak will guide her towards the stranger. No one else can protect her from the sheikh who wants her dead. Without the white streak on the horizon, she would wander until the end of time, spinning like the earth, not knowing which way to turn. She feels the child between her hips kicking her again and again, telling her she was right to leave Khouf, that there is no life there for her or her child. He urges her to flee, pushing her onwards when her legs can no longer carry her. She crawls up the slope on all fours, gripping at rocks and tufts of broom. Going back is out of the question. A vulture lurches towards her, mistaking her for a goat. She waits with eyes closed, terrified, unable to move, dreading the assault of the beak tearing at the back of her neck, bloodying her head. The vulture wants nothing less than to strip her flesh from her bones. Then it turns away, repelled perhaps by her woman's smell, the shadow of its giant wings vanishing into the distance with a long cry. She starts to climb again, determined to reach the plain before night, when wolves, badgers, coyotes and snakes come out of their lairs. She doubles her speed in spite of the wind whistling around her head, trying to silence it by blocking her ears with both hands. All her attention is focused on the road that leads to the father of her child, and on the child in a state of high excitement now that the summit is within sight.

The last three steps require a superhuman effort. Clinging to a rock, she manages to pull herself onto a ridge, lies down flat and stretches her limbs to ease the cramps in her legs; she would lie there all day if it weren't for the icy snow burning the skin on her back. From below, it seemed as if she would be able to touch her finger to the sky if she made it to this summit. She realises now that the sky is as far away as before.

The sun begins to sink rapidly, forcing her to get up. She looks behind her to check that no one is following her, and begins her descent of the other side. Her legs are too drained to keep a steady pace. Realising she has lost all control of her movements, she lets herself be dragged along by her own weight, knowing that the smallest mistake would throw her headfirst onto the jagged scree, that she would break her neck and die like the goats found rigid at the foot of the mountains, their glassy eyes still turned towards the summit.

Tumbling effortlessly down the mountain side, Noor

reaches the valley floor. The wind has dropped and she hears a chorus of low calls and harsh, grating cries. The gathering darkness rouses toads, jackals and wild boar from their slumber. Noor will not let herself rest, she sets off again, pushed onward by the child turning in her belly like a spinning ball. She sees a star between two branches. And soon another one, then more and more, lighting up as if to guide her as she moves forward.

She puts her trust in them even though she doesn't know their names, nor which way they point. She walks with her hands supporting her hips, the child like a stone deep in her belly. In the distance, a tree seems to be signalling to her with its single branch. Reaching the tree, she utters a deep sigh, slumps with her back against the trunk and sinks into an impenetrable slumber. No force on earth is strong enough to wake her. Does she dream the sheep that come to sniff at her, the dog barking and the old shepherd leaning over her? He sees her belly gripped by contractions, recites a *ta'wizat* and leaves her in hands of the Creator and of nature. They alone can deliver her. Crossing his arms and slapping his shoulders, he walks away to the sound of tinkling bells, knowing that he can do nothing to help her.

No one hears her cries but Noor herself. The mountain, now a dark shadow, sees nothing. The earth itself moves in her belly. It seems to her that her cries make the very air tremble, make the short grass and the single branch above her head shake. Blood and mucus spread around her. When the child's head appears between her thighs, she pulls it towards the outside, towards life, extricates it from her entrails. She cuts the cord with her teeth, lifts the baby up, checks that all is intact, and lays her baby on her breast, gazing long and hard at the child. A girl. Her baby is a girl, as fair as her brothers are dark. As dark as stone-baked bread, as the charred façade of the house she set fire to with her own hands.

That night, as you close your shutters, you see the image of a child in the face of the moon.

32.

Khouf buzzes with alarming rumours. They spill out through windows, slip beneath doors, erupt from holes in the ground, emerge from cracks in walls and fissures in the bark of trees. Even the call of the muezzin, his voice made hoarse by chill winds, carries whisperings. Talk that emanates from the city, travelling faster than Abdul's bus, further than the road linking the city to the desert, terrifying the children, turning their parents' hair white. Along the coast, revolt is in the air. People are hungry, demanding bread and meat. The aid agencies have left, moved on like a swarm of locusts, leaving poverty in their wake and taking good fortune with them. It's said that looters broke into bakeries and butchers' shops; finding nothing to put in their bellies, they directed their anger towards the thousand-year old stone lions that stand guard in front of the governor's residence, smashing them with hammers and bare hands. Books were suddenly considered suspect and suffered the same fate. Libraries and bookshops were set alight: what good is learning when it can't even provide people with the bare necessities? Thousands of books were reduced to ashes. The rioters warmed themselves on the flames, felt no pity for ancient manuscripts crackling in agony. Wild cavalcades the length and breadth of the residential districts could be heard all the way to Khouf, the sound of trampling feet, shouts ringing out all night long. Crowds hunting down the devil, the friend of the rich, dwelling in their homes. The devil, who hides in their safes, eats from their plates, impregnates their women, drives their cars.

One young fanatic thought he saw the devil in the outline of a cloud and scaled the mountain on horseback to slay him on the spot. The closer he drew to the devil, the further away his target seemed. Enraged, he turned against the earth itself, dug a hole, dug down further and called to Satan, commanding him to come out and fight man to man and let the stronger man win. People say all kinds of things in Khouf, anything their tongues will allow. One says that God is dead. The devil, claims another. God and the devil, says a third, look at all the troubles that have befallen Khouf. The mullah responsible for enforcing virtue has been deposed: he took it calmly, hailing the lineage of the Prophet and blowing first on his right shoulder then his left before setting off for home on foot. The Minister for the Suppression of Vice, renowned for his severity, recited a string of insults before he left the premises and walked off, taking his armchair with him.

The aging anchorite elevated to the position of leader soon appointed a first minister, under the novel title of Minister for Identifying Good and Evil. Newly empowered and determined to set the country to rights, he passed a new law every hour on the hour. His decrees were promptly enacted by uneducated officials, men deemed to be well-versed in matters of good and evil, capable of deciding who was a believer and who a heretic, of drawing the line between pure and impure, truth and untruth.

Decree number one: absolute segregation of men and women in every sphere, including cemeteries. Men to be buried on the right, women on the left, with odd numbers for men, even for women. The dead reunited not with their families, but with their own sex.

Decree number two: changes of vocabulary in current usage. Concepts and objects to be known by new designations in order to wipe the slate clean of the past. Cacophony ensued. Two names would be given to the same thing causing confusion and misunderstandings between members of the same family, with arguments flaring up like violent storms.

Decree number three forecasts nothing less than the end of the world.

Whether these decrees are real or invented by the people of Khouf, who have held a grudge against the city dwellers from time immemorial, they have done nothing to deflect the people from their obsession with the stoning of Noor, with the pile of stones waiting in the square for almost eight months.

'Her guilt measures no more than a quarter turn of the clockface', opines the only man in Khouf in possession of a watch.

'Her punishment should amount to no more than a bowlful of urine,' says the healer who speaks through the herbs she gleans from the mountains.

'The foreign woman is the one who should be stoned,' declares the qadi. 'Without her encouragement, Noor would not have dared to flee.'

'Amina is the guilty one, a witch who foresees only bad for the people of Khouf,' concludes the sheikh.

And one last pronouncement, neither decree nor rumour: 'A cockerel for the man who captures Noor,' proposes the barber.

'What good is a cock without a hen?' old Jalila crows. 'Males do nothing but strut about. It's the females who lay the eggs. In the chicken coop or in the shade of a tree if they have to.' She doesn't say if she means women or hens.

Noor, clasping her baby to her breast, looks at the tree above her for the first time. Its ragged meagre foliage will provide no protection for her. She sets off to look elsewhere for a roof over her head. Where should she go, which way should she turn? It all looks the same, in every direction. The sound of water draws her towards an embankment. She decides to put her faith in it. Water means a river and with the river, the dam, she tells herself, her heart rising in her chest, stopping her breath. Accustomed as she is to the thin stream that runs beside her Barbary fig, she is taken aback by the sight of so much water in one place. Is this really a river? It is so much broader, louder than she'd imagined. Now that she is so close to her goal, she is worried. Perhaps the man who planted the baby in her belly was only of her own imagining.

While she was pregnant, she was sure of him, but now the child has been thrust from her womb, she has her doubts.

The face of the man she loved while the *khamsin* clawed at them is veiled by fog, watered down by the blood she spilled giving birth.

Blood with the familiar dull, cloying smell, caked here and there on her dress, cracking now like the mud-brick walls in Khouf, like the walls of her house. Her blood and her home spilling out of her together.

Noor walks on, catlike, relying on instinct to guide her. She stops only to feed the child. And it is then, sitting on a rock, the little lips pressed to her breast, that she sees the dam. So close, and yet so far away, spanning the river that churns beneath her.

The banks cannot contain the raging waters that surge all around. She creeps stealthily towards the river, as if approaching a dangerous beast. Mist and spray obscure the features of the men working on the site. The sound of rushing water drowns out the orders shouted by the man directing the works. She recognises him in spite of the helmet. They lied to her when they told her he'd gone back to his own country, that the works had been halted by lack of funds. He is there, running from one group to another, calling out orders in that language of which she understands not a word. He is bigger than she remembers him, older than the man she yearns for, a man not of her race.

She has fallen into a trap. And so? Why be ashamed? She has been given a gift surpassing all her hopes, the flesh and blood she holds close to her breast is hers alone. She will share her daughter with no one. No man will claim paternity, no one will register her birth. Her child will be a citizen of no country, she will be the judge of her own life.

The men working on the other bank are suddenly lit by generous sunshine. Bare-chested and bronzed, their hair thick and dark, so unlike the pale silhouette of the man caught up in the swirling dust. Noor could touch him with her finger. All she has to do is wade through the clear shallow water. Something holds her back, a force independent of her will. She stands staring at the reeds swaying in the breeze, their image in the water a reflection of her life, limpid and murky at the same time. She has come all this way in search of a man: now that he is within her reach, she has chosen not to speak to him.

She turns her back on the dam, holds her daughter closer, afraid that she might slip from her breast.

33.

Every day, the numbers of would-be scholars dwindle. The children are bored at school. How can they concentrate with two voices, yours and the muezzin's, calling to them in different languages? You ask them to recite the alphabet, while he calls them to prayer. They don't like school, don't want to add and subtract. They'd rather sit astride a donkey, gulp down eggs in the chicken coop. Their legs are made for running, their little heads cannot hold two alphabets, their own is enough. The canniest have come up with a trick: they turn French words into Arabic words. *Abeille*, (bee) becomes *abaya*, *lampe* becomes *lamba*, *table tabla*, *jarre jarra*. Who cares if the meaning is not the same? It's the French words that must adjust, be more supple, more accommodating. You don't object, don't tell them they're wrong. You avoid correcting their mistakes for fear of humiliating them, but it irks you when *lapin* becomes *labin*, turning rabbit into yogurt, when *âne*, donkey becomes *aïn*, eye, and *herbe* becomes *harb*, turning grass into war.

You carry on teaching in spite of the hostile atmosphere and the suspicions that hang over you with regard to Noor. You helped her run away, you knew the stay of execution you'd extracted from the Minister for the Protection of Virtue would not last for ever. You went against the Sharia and its exhortation to end the life of an adulterous woman under a hail of stones.

By the end of the day, you feel discouraged, irritated by the ones that make no effort and annoyed with yourself for not managing to plant anything of your own language in their heads. The parcel that arrived this morning was another disappointment. Pencils, notebooks, rulers, you were happy with all of those, even the map of France, although a map of their own country would have been much better. You could have used it to teach them some geography, to show them that there is more to their land than Khouf, the desert and a mountain.

But what can you do with the New Testament sent by a well-meaning Catholic agency? The sight of those thirty volumes, the arms of the crucified martyr wrapped around their covers, leaves you in a state of bewilderment. Who should you give them to? You are not here to convert the children but to teach them to read, to add, subtract and multiply.

You have no desire to play the missionary, to tell them that there is another prophet, greater than theirs. To persuade them this other prophet is the son of God, when they know with certainty that Muhammad is Allah's messenger, the only one through whom God speaks. You unwrap the books, then put them back in the box. 'I'll do it tomorrow', you say to yourself, knowing that there are no certainties about tomorrow.

Your future in the *douar* is dependent on Noor, who has taken herself off to the hills, her back turned on the dam and the man constructing it. Light and free to do as she will, unburdened by the child that weighed so heavily in her womb, that now she carries, light as a feather, on her back. She walks with a spring in her step that says she's free, free for the first time in her life. She swings her body forward, letting the wind sweep her along, as if the wind had become her ally, her accomplice. It leads her to a bend in the river, where the water churns around as if in a bowl. She undresses, sinks into the water with her baby, indifferent to the streak of blood that turns the water red. Blood that will go on flowing from her, wherever she goes. She is not concerned. The blood darkened by all that she has suffered is leaving her, to be replaced by fresh blood, the colour of rubies.

There in the long grass that forms a protective wall around her and her child, Noor feels free of all danger, a thousand miles from Khouf, from the sheikh and the qadi, from Moha, the man who took her sons from her, stripped her house of door and windows. On reflection, she was right to destroy everything, to avenge her plants, her tomatoes, aubergines, courgettes and most of all her basil plant, her favourite, the one that held a special place in her heart, a place once occupied by a cat, lost one night when the *khamsin* blew, a cat she might have found if a stranger had not crossed her path and sewn the seed of his desire in her belly.

Noor feels as if she is on another planet, even the vegetation is not the same as in Khouf. No crops, no lentils or maize, only perfumed herbs, fruit trees. She only needs to reach up and pick the fruit and her thirst is quenched. The high wall of the mountain has cut her off from the squat palm trees of Khouf, from its eyeless houses, its cemetery dug into the sand and its unquiet dead. Theirs is the black breath that dries up the wells, that fractures the soil and makes the people cruel. The dead of Khouf are to blame for drought, for hunger and thirst. Old Jalila, loving no one and loved by none, is right to accuse them of sucking out all the water in the wells, of devouring the roots of all that men plant.

Her memories of Khouf are of a colourless place, darker than in reality. A place without flowers, except for the poppies, the devil's grass. Cut and dried on rooftops, ground to powder to become a drug, to furnish them with dreams. Even new-borns imbibe it, with a pinch in their bottle to calm their cries and lull them into a deep sleep.

34.

The desert has become a vast garden. Thousands of flowers have sprung up overnight. They'll bloom for three days, three weeks, no more, according to the experts. You close your door, reassured that Noor's fate is safe in the hands of nature. Lightning streaks across the sky as you turn out the light. Water rains down on Khouf, invisible hands pouring it over rooftops and along paths, transforming them into rivers of mud. You call out to Amina, needing to hear the sound of your own voice, to break the silence. Old Jalila appears, as if she was sleeping beneath your window. She foresees the worst. A deluge is approaching, nothing will stop the rain so long as Noor is alive. Adulterous women bring disaster. A woman who opens her *"firj"* to a stranger creates a breach in the sky. She must die. You push her outside and close your door. The morning brings a lull in the storm and the sound of hooves, so familiar since Rahim started coming to your school. He's braved the storm to bring you some good news. The engineer has come back, bringing money and new equipment with him. There will be work for everyone in the *douar*. A sad look comes over his face as his gaze falls on the bibles you received yesterday. He's seen the image of the crucifixion before, he's heard about Issa, the martyr, son of Sitt Maryam. Wasn't he crucified by the Yahouds?

You remind him that Christ was a Jew himself.

He rummages through the box, asks you if he can take one to give to the engineer. You say yes, but only if he gives him a letter from you.

'You know him?' he asks incredulously.

'Not really – no more than you know Christ. But he might know where Noor is. She hasn't been seen for two days.'

'You mean the woman who's going to be stoned? She's gone off by herself to wander Allah's paths? A woman alone, without husband, father or brother, is destined for a sorry end. Easy prey for murderers and wolves. Like a goat that's not tethered. My father says women are meant to live within four walls.'

You taste smoke rising in your throat, as if Rahim had set it on fire. Seeing he's upset you, he picks up a broom and begins to sweep the floor, but there is nothing to sweep up. He lapses into silence and you occupy yourself writing the letter to the man Rahim refers to as Sidi Engineer.

"Dear Sir", you begin on the blank sheet.

"Please forgive my intrusion into your private affairs, but I am compelled to do so on a matter of great urgency.

Three days ago, a woman disappeared from the *douar*. You met her, just over eight months ago, while she was searching for a lost cat. Your paths crossed during a windstorm. Perhaps you remember it. You were lovers, if I may put it that way. Her sons denounced her to the sheikh. She was accused of adultery and will be stoned after the birth of the child she is carrying. That child is yours. She believes in all innocence that you have not forgotten her and has gone in search of you, believing that you will protect her.

Is she with you? If she is, I beg you to send me word, by means of the person who has brought you this letter."

It is noon. None of the children from the *douar* or from the surrounding area have come to school. Rahim has gone on his way, leaving his donkey's hoofprints in the sand, and you fretting for Noor.

Perhaps, realising that one day their village will be drowned by the dam, the inhabitants of the *douar* have moved on and gone to other more welcoming sites.

They've fled while you slept, taking their children and their chickens with them, all bundled up together.

The sky hangs low on the horizon, ready to crush you, pushing you towards the square with its scattered shacks that pass for shops. You pace through the streets, ready to knock on every door and summon up your pupils. No sound filters through the narrow windows from the dimly lit interiors. The only signs of life come from the mosque. Childish voices repeat the same phrase, over and over again: *La ilaha illalah.*

The same litany until their throats run dry on the last judgment day. Young voices, echoed by the quavering tones of an old man, his voice like a candle-flame flickering in the wind.

The eternal melody of life in Khouf. In a flash you understand the reason for your pupils' absence. The sheikh has convinced them that only the *Kitab* can teach them anything of value.

You stop just beyond the last of the houses. Your westerner's feet have never trod the fields, let alone the desert. Nature is full of traps. You are not like Noor and Amina: they are of the earth, both vegetable and mineral, made of the same stuff as the tree bark and the sand. On the edge of the village, the air smells of foxes, of goat pelts wet from the rain, of the acidic tang of maize growing again for the first time in three years. The silky rustling of leaves makes it seem that Khouf is inhabited only by wind and water. Suddenly the voice of the muezzin rings out in the air, castigating women who rebel against the authority of men.

His words are aimed at you as much as at Noor.

You stand rooted to the spot, wondering if you should leave or stay to see this through to the end. Unable to make up your mind, you decide to ask Amina, to talk to her about it, even though she has been avoiding you for a while. She doesn't come and knock on your door any more, no longer shares her visions and hallucinations with you.

At night, you can tell where she is from the sound of her cooking pot as she moves it around, from the oaths she utters when the flame is reluctant to light. Is it Amina or the wind blowing through the cracks in the walls? Is it her, coughing, running the water even though she knows the water tank has almost run dry and that no one in the *douar* will come to the assistance of two women on their own? They will punish you, leave you to die of thirst for having helped Noor to escape the fatwa.

35.

The mud-spattered jeep braking violently outside the door matches Noor's description perfectly. A lithe long-legged man with eyes as grey as the sky extracts himself from the driver's seat. Dressed in boots and a ten-gallon hat, he looks more like a cowboy from a Texas rodeo than a civil engineer from Paris. He beckons to you with his index finger, puffs out his chest and without pausing to introduce himself holds out the letter you gave to Rahim, handling it with disgust, like a dead mouse.

'So you're the one who came up with this drivel, are you? Of course you are', he sneers, spitting on the ground. 'No one else in this shithole can write French.'

He looks you up and down, a sardonic smile on his fleshy lips. Then he bursts out laughing.

'Just what are you getting at here? Are you saying I took advantage of an innocent woman? That it's my fault the sheikh, the qadi and the whole pack of them want to stone her? Don't make me laugh! They should be thanking me, your sheikh and your qadi. A scrawny creature like her, the *khamsin* would have thrashed her against the wall. Little tart, claiming to be looking for a cat when all she really wanted was a man to screw her. I should have known better than to take pity on a bitch like that. I should never have taken her back to her house…'

'…after you raped her,' you interject, your voice as loud as his. 'Rape. That's what I call it. Noor says it was love.'

'Are you out of your mind? You seem to have forgotten, I'm a respectable married man, married to a real woman, not one of these bitches. Better off fucking a goat!'

Without waiting for you to react, he throws a hundred dirhams at you and drives off, saying that's all she's getting, not a penny more. The jeep's tyres carve through the mud on the road, streaking through your head. You don't move. You stand there, spattered in mud, wringing your hands, at a loss for what to do. The filth poured into your ears by Mr. Respectable Engineer will need a flood, a deluge worthy of Jalila's predictions to wash it away.

You hear footsteps approaching behind you but you're too weary to turn round. You've given up expecting any of your pupils or their parents. Jalila's voice floats towards you, a spider sending shivers down your spine; her words rise up on your shoulder, brush your cheek. She's trying to reassure you, telling you Noor has been seen, running along the river bank, singing like a mad woman, at the top of her voice. With a newborn on her back, reeking of blood. Noor, a mother cat with her kitten.

You should go back to your own country now, is Jalila's advice. Now that Noor has no more to fear, and Amina is staying away from you. Leave them to their fate, let them go back to being what they were before you came, *hourmas*, no different from goats. They'll manage without you. Noor and Amina are two faces of the same moon, destined to be eclipsed together. Two legs in one *sirwal*. Leave while there's still time, with your head held high, before you have to flee, before the stones piled up for Noor rain down on you.

36.

Every morning you walk along the *douar's* only street in search of the pupils you know will never come back to your school. You walk, eyes straight ahead; never on the passers-by nor on the women sitting in their doorways. To look at them would amount to meddling in their affairs, looking down on them. You would have stuck to your resolve if it hadn't been for the little girl who fell over in your path. You pick her up, sponge off her injured knee. She's ready to go but she raises her little arms to you, pleading to be carried. You head for the first door, bearing her slight body in your arms. A woman squats in the shade of a cactus hedge, just like Noor's, leaning over a steaming cauldron of boiling linen. She turns round, hearing the child's cries and your footsteps. Her veil falls back to reveal her gleaming hair, of the same gold as the girl's. She panics, fearing the worst and cries out in English: 'Oh god, oh my god, oh god!' She snatches the child from your arms and says: 'Thank you, thank you, love.'

Noor had told you about a young Irish woman who'd fallen in love and converted to Islam, hiding from her father for three months at the stud farm run by her beloved. Her father was an archaeologist digging up treasures in the desert, bones that he'd catalogue meticulously and send off to UNESCO's anthropology institute.

While he was busy digging, his teenage daughter would gallop around the *douar*, her hair blowing in the wind, its golden colour a stark contrast to the midnight black of the horse's coat. You were hoping for Noor to tell you the rest of the story, but she went off on a sidetrack about herself, saying she'd never envied the Irish woman even though she turned heads everywhere she went. Noor was a rich woman, she had no reason to complain. She had her goat and her own name, something that poor girl didn't have. She'd given up her name when she was married. Kirstin became Aïsha. The people of Khouf pretended to be looking for her, but they knew very well where she was. Her father went back to his country in despair, believing she'd been devoured by wild beasts.

His departure set tongues wagging. Kirstin came out of hiding, gave her man three children, all with hair the colour of rust, and freckles as numerous as the stars in the sky. The archaeologist still weeps for his daughter; he's never learned the truth. The people of Khouf say nothing, they're afraid of reprisals from the Irish ambassador. No one visits Aïsha-Kirstin, she might as well be dead. Is she happy? Who knows? She's never learned the language, talks to no one but her children, in English. She's content to communicate with her husband through gestures, nodding or shaking her head to make herself understood.

And now here you are, face to face with her in her small mud-brick house, no different from any other. Pots hanging on the wall glisten as they catch the light. On the opposite wall are two photos: a young woman, Aïsha-Kirstin, the other a white-haired man. She offers you a seat, thanks you again. The English words sound strange drifting through the smoke from the hearth, with the mattresses rolled up in a corner, verses from the Qur'an in exquisite calligraphy framed on the wall. Your gaze falls on a trunk and she explains that it holds everything her father left behind him, the fruits of a year's digs.

'He left it all here,' she says slowly. 'He didn't want to keep anything of the land that took his daughter from him.'

'Why have you never written to him?' you ask, surprising yourself with your own audacity.

Her answer comes like the crack of a whip: 'He wouldn't know me. Kirstin is no longer Kirstin. She's become Aïsha.'

You step out into the waiting night, a cloud of insects round your head. Slapping them away with both hands, you walk away, resolved to see no more of her.

37.

The rain, absent for so many years, refuses to loosen its grip on the *douar*. You awake to the sound of the downpour and open the door as you do every morning, convinced there will be no one there. But you see a figure, sitting on a case, careless of the rain falling in torrents all around. She sits, unmoving and unblinking, making no attempt to shelter herself from the downpour. The Irish woman looks up at you, water streaming down her face. She points to the case, the same one you saw yesterday. She asks you to take it back to its owner, the name and address are written inside the lid, the phone number too. You tell her that transporting archaeological artefacts requires official documentation. She won't hear of it. You are her friend, the only one she has here, you brought her child back to her, crossed her threshold. In a bitter voice, words jostling with each other to spill out faster, she speaks of her guilt at having kept her father's collection when she had no right to do so. They are a burden to her, bringing suffering to her and her husband.

Bones of the dead, long dead, raining bad luck down on them, stifling their lives. Saïd has not advanced in his work at all. Their children are constantly falling ill. She cleaned her daughter's knee thoroughly with alcohol, but still it's infected.

'The dead of the desert want none of us', she crows. What she says next leaves you speechless: 'I never got back on a horse. I've done my penance. And there's still no end to my father's sorrows.'

She doesn't wait to see the effect of her words. Aïsha-Kirstin strides off, straight and tall, the rain lashing down all around her.

38.

How fickle Jalila is. Two days ago, she held Noor and Amina in equal scorn. Today Noor is forgotten, and Jalila is full of concern for Amina.

'No wonder she's gone funny in the head', she explains, all sympathy and understanding. 'Poor girl was born on the wrong side of the day, at dusk, between sun and moon, when shadows are long and cats keep their paws close to the walls. I should have kept her in my belly for an hour longer.'

'You mean she's your daughter?' you gasp, dumbfounded by this revelation.

'She was, until you showed up. She started following you around and suddenly she was ashamed of her old mother. Told me she didn't want to be seen with me, won't even let me say hello. Amina won't be Jalila's daughter again until you've packed up and gone and Noor's been finished off by the stones. And now, with that sinful woman vanished into thin air, they'll go after my daughter. Those stones have to be used for something.'

You're probably safe from the stones, she points out, seeing you grow pale, for the simple reason that they wouldn't know what to do with your body. There's no place for heretics in the Khouf cemetery. The *turbas* of Khouf are reserved for the faithful.

Jalila blows hot and cold, striking terror into your heart while pretending to set your mind at rest.

'You're a foreigner, they won't touch a hair on your head. But they will humiliate you, they'll hound you from the *douar* with sticks and stones.'

Changing the subject without warning, she asks you what Saïd's wife wanted this morning. What was in the suitcase? Infuriated by your silence, she goes on to say she's convinced the Irish woman wants to get away from Khouf, to leave her husband and children. She'll get you to send on her things and then she'll slip away unnoticed, back to her own country and all the food she can eat.

This woman is the very devil, you say to yourself, aghast. You close your eyes to put her out of your sight. Her voice drifts towards you from afar, telling you to have a good cry and clear your head, to get something to eat and put some flesh on your bones, you're scrawny as a chicken, a puff of air could knock you over. Noor and Amina have worn you out. Jalila will look after you. Jalila's done nothing wrong. Jalila didn't beat you. She didn't spit in your face. All she did was rain a few words no bigger than hailstones on you. You only have yourself to blame, going to pieces over the slightest little thing. It's your problem if you've lost your tongue, your problem if you've swallowed a bee.

39.

Now that Noor's gone, taking her swollen sinner's belly with her, people have turned their venom on me. Amina, the corrupter of souls, evil incarnate, casting spells in the four corners of the earth, right and left, one for every finger of each hand. Amina, the maker of charms, with neither string nor scissors to cut the threads that hold them together. Noor hides in the bowels of the mountain, the desert has closed behind her, burying her footprints in the sand. She's freed herself from the confines of her cactus hedge, escaped the clutches of the people who watched over her every move. They're still looking for her. Some say they've seen her gesticulating in the branches of a palm tree, others claim they've heard her talking to the qadi's nightingale inside its cage. Or else they've seen her image reflected in the water, even though the water's all gone from Khouf; she's masquerading as a cloud, sticking her tongue out at them, taunting them from her vantage point, beyond the reach of anyone trying to silence her. No one has a ladder high enough to reach the sky.

With Noor out of the picture, the muezzin aims his barbs

at the witch. "*Kazaba al mounajjimoun.*" Fortune-tellers have spoken falsely, says the Book of Books. I'm no fortune-teller, I just read coffee grounds like some people read the paper. And then during the last azan of the day, I decided I'd shout louder than he does. Protected by the darkness I called him a liar, accused him of overstepping himself, only the sheikh is authorised to recite verses, he'd do better stick to chanting "*Allahu Akbar*" in that grating voice of his that pierces the air and makes it grimace.

With Noor's skin beyond their reach, they're trying to get their hands on me. But it's no sin to read coffee grounds, it gives a woman something to do with her time. A way for me to earn a bit of money now the aid workers have gone and the Centre's been turned into a school for ignoramuses. I do it in a flash, in less time than it takes them to read the alphabet. If I hesitate they think it means something unpleasant, a death or bad news of some kind. They pay me to give them hope. I tell the poor they'll make a fortune, I foresee marriage for single women, tell battered wives they'll soon be widowed. I don't open my mouth unless I can make someone happy. The muezzin refuses to believe in my good faith. Five times a day, from the top of his minaret, he lays into witches: "*Kazaba al mounajjimoun*". Words that no one but the sheikh is supposed to say, but he lets the muezzin get away with it.

"Fortune-tellers have spoken falsely": his voice startles the drowsy morning sun, the steely blade of the midday sun and the dying evening sun alike. A voice full of hate, a voice that names no names but points to those who lead their fellow men astray *with false predictions.*

"We have prepared a fitting punishment for them, they will be brought low. We shall cast them into oblivion."

The muezzin's words are aimed at astrologers too, not just at Amina, reading the coffee grounds in exchange for a handful of dates and a bowl of chorba. His voice follows me everywhere I go, even to the warehouse. I should have been more careful that day I found Noor waxing her belly. Only young brides are meant to do it, not pregnant women, wineskins full of blood ready to gush forth with every hair pulled out.

I can't ask the foreign woman to protect me: she's too busy trying to turn little cretins into founts of knowledge. She gets attached to them – she'd be better off tethering them to the nearest palm tree like Rahim's donkey and giving them bread instead of slates and chalk.

"Fortune tellers have spoken falsely." The muezzin wants me dead. The pile of stones prepared for Noor will end up falling on my head. Yesterday I climbed to the top of the palm tree, led by instinct. Quite a performance. In no time at all I was perched at the same height as him. I yelled at him, voice rasping like a rusty saw, like a wheel stuck in the mud. I told him to come down onto solid ground and stand next to me, Amina who has done nothing wrong Do you know what he did? Coward that he is, he pretended he hadn't heard and turned his crow's face and his bad breath towards the mountain as if he were accusing the rocks themselves of lying.

I'd shinned up the tree as nimbly as a date-picker and came back down to earth a changed woman. People saw me running around in the fields for fear of coming across my fellow beings and said I'd gone mad. Amina, once so submissive, full of rage now. Withered ears of corn rose up as I passed and cried "Fortune tellers have spoken falsely". Brambles uttered the same words, even the sparse rough grasses stood to attention and cried: "Burn the witch, burn her now, what are you waiting for?" The one frog that survived the drought joined in too, not to be outdone, opening and closing his mouth soundlessly. I ran on, not stopping, for fear of being caught by the voices, running day and night, faster than the trees, the brambles, the grass and the frog, searching for myself, wasting away in front of their eyes, becoming more and more transparent, like a pane of glass, invisible, elusive, impossible to find. When the mob comes to search the foreign woman's school, there'll be nothing to hide.

But I still have this to say: there's a price to pay for the pain and suffering heaped on me since the aid workers left. Allah, who rights all wrongs, will make me a saint. I shall be as great as Sitt Zinab with a well twice as big as hers and water flowing freely. The people of Khouf, starting with the muezzin will kneel to drink there, they'll thank me, touching their forehead to the ground, three times, over and over again until they don't know which way is up.

40.

First Noor left and now Amina too has gone, leaving you more alone than ever. As the fifth prayer of the day ends and forty lanterns are lit, you prefer to think of your two friends far away from Khouf, from the sheikh and the qadi. For you know that Amina will be unable to find the words to defend herself. Making predictions or hurling insults comes easily to her, but she will bow her head like a lamb to the slaughter and offer no resistance to the execution-er's blade. With Noor gone, wandering somewhere in the wilds, Amina will take her place, although she has com-mitted no adultery. The night before she left, she asked you if she could sleep in your room, at the foot of your bed. You said yes. As Noor's only friends, you both feared for the same thing. Curled up on the bare floor she jumped at every sound, every time the wind slammed against the shutters. When dawn came, she made straight for the path to the fields where the vegetation had grown lush since the last rains. She was going to meet Noor, to share her fate, innocent as she was. Noor swooned in pleasure and gasped for breath in the arms of a man but Amina had felt nothing when Gonzagues rubbed himself up against her. She let him do it. She was doing him a favour, nothing more.

Amina is out of reach, but rumours from the *douar* are still directed at her. The muezzin, his voice full of hate, still aims his accusations at her, without invoking her name. She crosses the plain and stands at the edge of the desert, fearing its naked emptiness. Every shadow can be seen. She huddles close to the ground to walk, all but crawling over the damp sand.

She reaches the mountain with a sigh of relief. She has always known it from afar, never this close. Her will to join Noor gives her wings, she leaps recklessly from rock to rock, gripping at the smallest of handholds to haul herself up to the summit. 'I will find Noor', she mutters, her lips blue from exertion. Stones screech past her head, she is flung to the ground. Someone is following her.

Amina crawls on her belly towards a fissure in the rock, she curls in on herself, a ball of fear and sweat. The uncoiled snake confronting her prepares to attack. Transfixed with fear, she makes no attempt to escape. She stares with dazed eyes at the grey underbelly, counting the diamond-shaped markings. Does it feel her fear? The snake makes as if to strike, coils back on the ground and slithers off into a crack in the rock.

Amina takes up her walk again, her legs moving as if by

miracle. 'I will find Noor', she proclaims, loudly this time, her words heard and echoed by the mountain for the people of Khouf to hear. Her voice comes back to her, intoxicating her as it resounds in her ears. She calls out again: Amina is not a witch. Amina is a good woman. The visions she sees are dictated by benevolent spirits, not by evil ones. Amina has never hurt anyone. She is harmless, just a little funny in the head as her mother the beggar would say.

Amina thinks she is shouting but she cannot get the words out. All that comes from her lips is white vapour, her breath chilled by the iron cold that holds these heights in its grip.

With the wind whistling in her ears, she walks on. A wind that is nervous on the cliff edges, shrill when it catches its feet in the brambles, silent as it brushes against the vulture. She walks on, not pausing to rest, she must find Noor before nightfall, before the dam. Before the engineer gets back to the site. He would close the door on her, stop Noor from answering her call. Perhaps he will kill her, get rid of her, bury her in a block of concrete and leave no trace of her. Everyone knows the Frenchies have no mercy, they're not like Muslims with the fear of Allah inscribed in their hearts.

When she treads the summit beneath her feet, Amina knows she is out of danger. A harsh dry world surrounds her in every direction, blank and wasted, unsullied by man's hand. She would like to linger there, but duty calls her down, on both sides of the green line that snakes between two stands of trees, on one of the river banks that she must keep in sight if she is to find Noor. She knows the descent will be child's play after the climb. She will let her weight carry her, she will tumble effortlessly down to the valley. All that matters is that she arrives at the site before night-fall, before work stops for the day.

41.

The men of Khouf have gathered in the square for the last prayer of the day. They have decided to take action. Their authority is at stake. They will punish any *hourma* who leaves the *douar* without a man's permission. Like hunters stalking their prey, they skirt the mountain, probe its every cavity, explore every cavern, shout into all its fissures. With only their own echo for response, they wipe the sweat from their brows and look around. From a distance, their mountain always seemed grey, but under foot, it is white. White and crumbling like chalk or salt. Should they believe those who say the desert was originally a sea, that the *khamsin* covered it with sand, that the ships and the fish were replaced by caravans and camels? Once the sun had drunk the last drop of water, prattling winds whipped up the earth, flattening dunes and amassing them in one great monolith, a mountain that looked grey from the *douar*, white underfoot. A white so dazzling they forget why they are there, forget the woman they are pursuing.

Noor or Amina, the name matters little. They must assert their authority. What will become of them if their wives, daughters, mothers begin to seek pleasure elsewhere, if strangers take to mounting them, riding them bareback like mares without halter or saddle?

Alerted by a sound, Amina listens. No snake this time, but a man, his breathing laboured from running, from the effort of catching up with her. She closes her eyes, wills herself to remain still, he won't see her if she doesn't look at him. A loose trouser leg flies over her head, moves away and comes back towards the rock fissure she's slipped into to escape him. A pair of glowing embers peers into her narrow hiding place, searching. A triumphant cry rings out, laughter, like a hyena confronting carrion. A rallying cry to the hunters scattered over the slopes of the mountain, listening for the call to come together and claim their prize. Sticks probe the crack in the rock, stabbing blindly, not knowing if the prey is an animal or a woman, beating her into submission. They pull her out by the hair, crush her with their boots. They kick but do not punch, for they will not touch this abject body with their hands. Her face bloodied, her features deformed by their blows, the woman who came so close to escaping them still breathes. Have they caught Noor? Is it Amina? They cannot say. Night has come early and the mountain is plunged into darkness. They'll know when they get back to Khouf, to the square where the sheikh, the qadi and the whole *douar* are waiting.

Held fast in an iron grip, Amina is dragged over the

rocks, her body bouncing, almost flying, the pain intensifying until she no longer feels anything. Amina has become a nightingale.

After the rugged mountain slope, the plane is more merciful, a silken sheet around her bones. She lets herself slide along, more dead than alive. Does she recognise the square in Khouf? Seeing nothing, she hears the crowd chanting, the words *Allahu Akbar* a balm to her spirit, as soothing as the honeyed tones of the sheikh who greets her with the words: 'We shall make you a martyr, Noor, now that you have paid for your sin. We shall honour you every evening, as the sun goes down, after the last *azan* when the voice of the muezzin has fallen silent. The stones in the square can be removed now that Khouf has regained its dignity. Allah in his mercy accepts your repentance.'

'All has been done as it should', the qadi adds. 'We have heard the four witnesses to adultery as the Sharia requires. The three sons of the penitent and a fourth whose identity we shall not yet reveal.'

Amina has come closer to death with every step taken by the men dragging her. Now she is no more. Her eyes are open, but there is no one behind the gaze; her colourless empty tears are not the tears of the living. She is dead, like a tree, cut down branch by branch, weakening gradually with each assault on the bark, falling heavily under the final blow.

42.

Shouts and sounds of ululations propel you towards the square. Jalila stops you on the way, and warns you to leave Khouf before you find yourself caught up in events you cannot control.

'If you don't want to end up like the other one.'

Who the "other one" is she doesn't say.

You ask her if she means Noor or Amina and she answers with another question:

'Who can say? The dead are all alike. Once they've buried her, they could go after you. Save yourself while their attention is elsewhere. They've never liked you, never accepted you. No one trusts you, young or old. You have one mouth, but you speak with two tongues, Arabic to lull them into security, French to hide what you really think. If it weren't for you, Noor would have been lying beneath the stones for several moons now, Amina would still be reading coffee grounds in exchange for a bowl of *chorba*. You filled their heads with ideas, made Noor believe she was entitled to love, let Amina think she could foretell the future. They thought they were women like you instead of the females they are, sisters of all those who give birth, who calve and whelp.

'Leave and let us hear no more of you. Your friends are gone, dead one to the other. No life for Amina without Noor and no life for Noor without Amina. They were like two fingers of one hand.'

She crosses her fingers to underline her words. Two dried twigs covered in papery skin. Night blankets everything in its path. The table and bed are no longer visible, but you don't turn on the light. This evening, you are afraid of everything. The shadow of the palm tree on the sand forms the outline of a giant spider. Above your head you hear sounds that remind you of fierce ululations, tongues flapping furiously against the roof of the mouth. The gutter moans, rumbles, demands vengeance. Three taps on the window fill you with mad hope. You run over to it, ready to open the window and find Amina or Noor, both of them perhaps, alive in spite of what is being said, in spite of the crowd that formed around the dying woman in the square.

The person telling you to come and join her is none other than Aïsha-Kirstin, the lantern at her feet lighting up her pale face. Abdul has parked his vehicle just outside the *douar* so you won't be seen. 'He's arranged everything so you can leave without anyone noticing', she says to you for the third time.

You won't go without seeing Noor and Amina first.

What will become of them without you? She puts her hand to her mouth to silence you. Walls in Khouf absorb every word. Nothing is to be trusted. Starting with the qadi, an insomniac who paces the streets of the *douar* until dawn, and Jalila who sleeps with her back to the nearest wall. Abdul will not let them kill you, she mutters, her voice rasping with fear. It had never occurred to you that they would kill you. They would imprison you, use you as a bargaining chip for rice, flour, tins of food. France will demand your release, for form's sake.

You will be their hostage. You will pay the price for your colleagues who left without paying a visit to the sheikh, as if they were leaving a pigsty.

Leave while your legs can still carry you and while Abdul feels responsible for you.

'But what about my pupils?'

Aïsha-Kirstin bursts out laughing.

'The weak ones will become mujahideen, the violent ones, terrorists, and those that can preach and fire up the crowds will be imams.'

'I need to leave a key for Amina. She might come back. Who can I leave it with?'

'She won't be needing it, not after the beating she's taken', she says in a hoarse whisper.

'You mean it's not Noor dead in the square?'

Aïsha-Kirstin waves her hand over her shoulder in response. She does not want to know. You start stuffing things into a bag, ready to leave.

Kirstin leaves you after she has delivered you to Abdul, to become Aïsha once again beneath the veil that covers her from head to foot.

You follow in Abdul's footsteps, his lantern illuminating the straggly palms. They look like upturned brooms. The din in the square has been replaced by silence. Have they gathered behind closed doors somewhere to discuss what to do with you? Abdul doesn't like this silence. He urges you to walk faster. Beneath your feet the earth is red, the sand on the edge of the desert seems tinged with blood. Abdul closes the door, starts up the bus gently. Seated at the back of the bus, you are the sole passenger. Your conversation takes place over fifteen rows of empty seats. Questions and answers don't always match, but you don't care. You feel safe with him, the two of you united in your unconsummated marriage, talking like an old couple. Like friends, partners in crime.

'Where are you taking me, Abdul?'

'Somewhere where men have hearts and trees cast shadows.'

'How can I find out what's happened to Noor?'

'A woman nursing an infant is protected by her child's hunger.'

'She's had her baby?'

'Rocks don't give birth, don't bleed. The trail of blood from the dam to the road is the blood of a woman in childbirth.'

'Why not head for the dam?'

Abdul shakes his head.

'Blood flows with the one who bleeds, like water in a stream. Trees cannot walk. Trees spend their lives in one place, faces fixed in one direction.'

'So Noor is alive?'

'As alive as you or I.'

'And the woman they brought down from the mountain?'

'Amina, wearing Noor's clothes. Who knows why she borrowed that dress? Did she want to die for her? Allah alone knows.'

Abdul turns towards you in the darkness, unable to see your face.

'How many children have you brought into the world, foreign woman?'

'I used to have a cat', you splutter uneasily. 'He's gone.'

'Left, like Noor's husband? Maybe your cat will open a casino and make lots of money...'

Gloomy Abdul laughs uproariously, pleased to have come up with such a joke. He declares that the day will come when you will have as many children as the stars in the sky, no doubt to reassure you.

He can't know he's touched upon something, a deep-felt longing you've had for years. You wanted to have a child with your lover, but the thin stream of blood between your legs dashed your hopes at the end of every month. Blood from your heart.

He wouldn't have left me if he'd been happy with me,

you muse aloud. Abdul, still thinking of the cat, doesn't agree. Cats are not to be trusted, he says, you never know what they're going to do next. Faithless creatures that leave and come back, only to leave again.

The bus trundles noisily on through sleeping villages, rousing them from their slumber. The morning sun casts its harsh light on a tip, a mountain of rubbish standing ready for the children who come to scavenge. Abdul drives you through outlying districts, where people driven from their villages by hunger live piled up on one another. Birds fly from barren fields but fish never leave the sea. There is always food near the coast, even beneath the rows of tin roofing and lines of tattered clothing hung out to dry. A city beyond the city, surrounding and suffocating it. A city whose existence you'd been unaware of last time you came to the capital, when you thought you'd saved Noor from death. But all you'd done was delay it, passing the sentence to Amina, "born on the wrong side of the day, between sun and moon, in the mist, like her life," as Jalila said.

The sheikh and the qadi can sleep soundly now that a woman has died in the square. The stones are still there, stones piled up by the people of Khouf. People who are stronger now than before, forgotten by the state. Far away from the capital, the people of Khouf do not submit to the laws of the republic. Khouf belongs to the desert. Its people are not like the city dwellers who struggle to gain power and riches. They have other things on their minds. Their battle is against the sand that seeps into their huts, against the *khamsin* that keeps them trapped in their houses like rats, against the drought that saps their wells dry. The laws of the republic hold no sway in Khouf.

43.

When you arrived in Khouf more than eight months ago, your heart sank at the sight of children scrabbling in the earth in search of seeds. You were on a mission to help a doomed people, but you found yourself caught up in cruel practices, a legacy of medieval times. Instead of food, you offered them rebellion. First you, then Amina, were dragged into Noor's misfortune. You were saved by the Irish woman and by the people's reluctance to bury you in their cemetery. And by Abdul who has brought you aboard his bus that lurches and jolts like your life.

His eyes, reddened with fatigue, are lit up in the driving mirror by the first rays of the morning sun bursting into life.

'If Noor is safe, as you say, who is the dead woman in the square?'

Abdul says he doesn't know her name, but he heard her cries. He'd never heard such howling, neither animal nor human, but something between the two. The battered face was no one's. Certainly not Noor's.

'Do you know Amina?'

Abdul shakes his head. He only knows the people who use his bus, the woman was unrecognisable. She'd ceased to be a woman. They trampled her underfoot, carried on even after she was dead. Her mouth and nose were gone, but the eyes, wide open, continued to see.

Tears run down Abdul's cheeks as he drives the bus across a bridge over a dried up riverbed.

You see the nameless, faceless woman from the square in Khouf running between the cars, a dark shadow leaping from roof to roof, Amina's features beginning to emerge. You beat your fist against your chest, willing the shattered woman to be someone else, not Amina.

Distress has clouded your vision. You would do well to return to your own country. You will go mad if you carry on being obsessed with these two women. As mad as you were the day you decided to join the aid workers knowing that you were not cut out for this kind of work, simply because a man had left you for his wife, and your cat had left you for paradise. You were in such distress you chose the poorest country in the world, a village spat out on the edge of the desert, where the palm trees are as misshapen as the camels and the sheikh is a despot who rules by terror. Your exile had hinged on the cat. If he'd lived you would never have met Noor, or Amina or Abdul, and certainly not the sheikh, who married you and Abdul for a handful of coins. Marriage by *mutah*, of all marriages the most degrading, to a father of sixteen children running barefoot in the streets of a town destroyed first by war and then by earthquake.

Abdul drives you through districts that have never been rebuilt. No one has reconstructed the fallen buildings. No one has cleared away the rubble, it has simply been piled up at the sides of the road to allow taxis filled with tourists to feast their eyes on the spectacle and take photos.

Abdul likes to be the tourist guide, identifying the streets and the stalls that line them. Pharmacy, bookshop, cinema, restaurant, hotel. He is eager to share what he sees with you, but your thoughts are elsewhere. You cannot stop thinking about the dead woman in the square. What was she doing in the mountains? Why did the men of Khouf drag her down its slopes before kicking her to death? No oil left in her lamp, Abdul offers in explanation. You look unconvinced and he tries another proverb: "The Creator's permission must be given before a single hair on her head can be harmed." Always bowing to the hand of fate. Bristling with rage you wonder who this Creator is who hands out oil without rhyme or reason, who lavishes gifts on some and refuses them to others. Abdul's voice falls silent with the engine. He stops the vehicle and says no more. The Abduls of this world don't question the established order. Their faith doesn't spring from mystical revelation. It is a collection of beliefs handed down through the ages, which they make no attempt to change, either from inertia or laziness. He thrusts his hands into his pockets, searching for something, and pulls out a photo which he holds out to you over his shoulder. A man with a bullet belt strung across his chest brandishing a Kalashnikov to the sky. It's Abdul. He'd fought in the mountains, fired at planes that were diving straight at him, their bombs sending men, trees and rocks up in flames. Friends, comrades buried by night, if they weren't blown to pieces. They would bury an arm, a leg, sometimes only a finger, and then pray. They couldn't just leave them to the wolves and the snow.

You gaze from the photo to the shattered buildings, collapsed in on themselves, one floor falling in on another. Thick vegetation grows inside the bedrooms. An army of gaunt cats battles against hordes of plump rats, carrying on the war where the men left off.

'We'll rebuild, we'll be born anew', he mutters beneath his moustache.

You hand him back the photo, hoping against hope that Amina too will be reborn one day.

44.

As the bus turns a corner the Home for Widows and Orphans looms grey and solid. Abdul opens the door for you, helps you find your footing, gives you a reassuring smile. You hand him a coin, the correct amount for the trip. He takes a step back, shakes his head and turns his back on you. He treads angrily in your shadow on the tarmac. He helped you as a friend and you've responded by treating him as no more than the bus driver. His silence is louder than words. He has nothing more to say to you and leaves you to make your way into the building alone. You've become a stranger to him. "All those not born here are strangers", goes the local saying. Perhaps he sees you as one of the "Russkies" who devastated his country. Alone in the middle of the road, surrounded by the honking of cars, hawkers shouting, the din of carts, you struggle to cross.

Three women stand in the doorway, giggling into their hands as you dither on the doorstep.

'Guess who's waiting for you inside', they exclaim all

at once.

Seeing you at a loss, the youngest of the three tries to help and urges you to give up.

'I give in. Who is it?' you ask obediently, your gaze coming to rest straight in front of you.

Leaning on the doorframe, a baby on her hip, is Noor.

'How did she get here?' you ask, your head spinning.

Three answers are fired at you by the three sisters all talking at once. You have to sort the truth from the fantasies.

'She walked here', claims one. 'She walked non-stop for a week.'

'No', says another, cutting her short. 'She'd have died if a man with a cart hadn't taken pity on her and her child. He loaded her up between two bags of lentils.'

'They're both wrong', says the eldest. 'They don't know what they're talking about. She's here because Abdul helped her, may Allah bestow his blessings upon him. That man deserves to go to paradise, with the forty virgins promised by the Prophet.'

Strangely, Noor accepts all three versions as true. Noor, like water filling a vessel, putty ready to be moulded, like the palm trees in Khouf, bowing to the will of the winds that blow from the desert.

Whether she walked, came here by cart or by bus, what does it matter? The miracle is that she is here, with her baby, presenting it to you. Without you, foreign woman, her lips are saying, the baby would be buried with her mother under a pile of stones. She holds the child out to you and says:

'Keep her, if your heart wills it. She's a girl. Her name is Basilia.'

Does she really mean it?

She insists, thrusts the child into your arms.

A gift, both magical and confusing. The smell of milk mixed with baby hair fills your nostrils. Motherhood, thrust upon you, in the form of a child you have neither carried nor given birth to. You sob, not knowing why. Ample-breasted women encircle you, put their arms around your shoulders, rub your back with their sturdy hands, swaddling you with warm affectionate words, consoling you. Someone wipes your eyes with the hem of her skirt, dabs your nose. Noor's woes are over, they tell you, she has nothing more to fear. The Minister for the Suppression of Vice has been deposed, sent back where he belongs. He could be dangling from the end of a rope for all anyone knows. You already know all this, but you pretend to be surprised, to make them happy. They talk for the sake of talking, hopping from one subject to another, always coming back to the baby clinging to you in your arms. Her features sharp like her mother's, eyes of the same green, the same golden skin.

'You are her second mother', they say for the hundredth time. 'Keep her until she gets used to you, while Noor goes back to the *douar* to replant everything that Moha ripped out. First, the basil plant, but most of all her flowers, blossoms to laugh in the face of drought, heat waves and cold, all the flowers in creation.' Basilia roots around, seeking your breast, hungry for her feed. They urge you to go through the motions. A hand slips a bottle between your fingers, another helps you to sit down, props up your back with cushions, takes off your shoes and slips your feet into soft *babouches*. The women fuss over you, as they would any mother of a newborn. A square of sweet *loukoum* slipped into your mouth to take the acidity from your milk, a glass of almond juice to make your milk flow freely. Two drops of orange blossom essence for colic, and a potent sleeping draft, infusion of poppy seeds.

45.

You are woken in the night by a child's cries coming from the room at the back where Noor sleeps with her baby. You get up, worried. No one else is awake. You feel your way in the darkness, trying to avoid the mattresses spread out on the floor, sometimes stepping on the bodies curled up asleep. No one seems to mind. You find the little bundle, almost choking on her own screams. You take her in your arms and she quietens instantly. You breathe in Basilia's unmistakeable smell, take in the green of her eyes, shining in the dark. You grope around in search of Noor. The woman you wake is not pleased, tells in you in a voice thick with sleep to go back to your mattress and not waste your time looking for Noor. She's left, gone home.

'Home? Where?'

'To Khouf, to her husband, who'll take her back, and make her the Queen of her own home again. Zahi, Zad, Zein will have their mother restored to them and the foreigner's daughter will leave the country. She wanted to say her farewells to you but she had to hurry, since Abdul's bus always leaves at midnight. Now that Noor is no longer pregnant, Moha will marry her again, without any fuss. She'll be free to tend her garden, plant her basil again, her tomatoes and courgettes. And possibly flowers too, why not? Blooms that have no fear of drought or frost. Now that the fatwa has been carried out on the other one, the way is clear for Noor. The stones had to take a woman's life. It mattered little who she was. Blood has been shed in the square in Khouf, the stones can be scattered again. One *hourma* has paid with her life for another's. Nothing to make a fuss about. Allah the most merciful and compassionate will redress the balance.'

About the Author

Vénus Khoury-Ghata is an acclaimed Lebanese poet and novelist. Born in 1937, she has been resident in France for many years. She is the author of numerous novels and collections of poetry and has been awarded, among other prizes, the Grand Prix de l'Académie Française and the Prix Goncourt de la Poésie, given in recognition of her life's work. Her poetry has been translated into many languages. *Seven Stones* is the first of her novels to be published in English.

About the Translator

Aneesa Abbas Higgins is a London based writer and translator. She studied French, Russian and Sociology at the Universities of Sussex and London and was a teacher for many years before becoming a translator. Her translation of the Goncourt-winning *What Became of the White Savage* by François Garde (Dedalus, 2015) was the winner of a PEN Translates award.